"We've got meat-eaters," Zed said. Then he muttered something about always being afraid this would happen someday.

"Did I miss a manual?" Elle asked.

Beside her Jay really looked puzzled.

Elle only shrugged, not knowing what to tell him yet.

It was as if the phone line had been cut. After a moment Elle said, "Hey, boss, this ain't helping us here."

"Sorry," Zed said. "Just pulling up a deeply classified file."

Elle shuddered. The entire MiB organization was so classified that no government on the planet even knew it existed. Every day before lunch it learned, and kept, secrets that could destroy the planet. Elle didn't want to know what kind of problem would need special classification in the MiB system, but she was about to find out anyway.

"Get back into the car," Zed said, "and I'll fax you the entire file."

The phone clicked off and Elle handed it back to Jay.

"Well?" Jay asked.

Elle shrugged and turned toward the car. "The big guy was making no sense. Something about meat-eating trees and a top secret file."

"Top secret?" Jay asked. "For MiB?"

"Yeah," Elle said. "Weird, huh?"

"Wow," Jay said. "I really don't think I want to know what that might be."

"We got no choice, good-lookin'," Elle said. "We're getting the fax."

THE GREEN SALIVA BLUES

Dean Wesley Smith

BANTAM BOOKS

New York   Toronto   London   Sydney   Auckland

MEN IN BLACK: THE GREEN SALIVA BLUES

A Bantam Book/June 1999

All rights reserved.
Copyright © 1999 by Columbia Pictures Industries, Inc.
All rights reserved.
Cover art copyright © 1999 by Columbia Pictures Industries, Inc.
All rights reserved.

No part of this book may be reproduced or transmitted in any
form or by any means, electronic or mechanical, including
photocopying, recording, or by any information storage and
retrieval system, without permission in writing from the publisher.
For information address: Bantam Books.

If you purchased this book without a cover you should be aware
that this book is stolen property. It was reported as "unsold and
destroyed" to the publisher and neither the author nor the
publisher has received any payment for this "stripped book."

ISBN 0-553-57768-9

Published simultaneously in the United States and Canada

Bantam Books are published by Bantam Books, a division of Random
House, Inc. Its trademark, consisting of the words "Bantam Books"
and the portrayal of a rooster, is Registered in U.S. Patent and
Trademark Office and in other countries. Marca Registrada. Bantam
Books, 1540 Broadway, New York, New York 10036.

PRINTED IN THE UNITED STATES OF AMERICA

OPM   10   9   8   7   6   5   4   3   2   1

For Kris, with love and thanks.

And for Janie and Jason Kiser.
It has been a pleasure watching you two
show your father and me just how old we really are.

*Blues actually is around you every day.
That's just a feeling within a person,
you know. You have a hard time and
things happen.*

—ARTHUR LEE WILLIAMS

The meek may inherit the earth, but not its mineral rights.

—JOHN PAUL GETTY

Spring had finally come to the small town of Greenwell, Connecticut, like the final stages of defrosting an old refrigerator. All the ice and snow had long since melted, and most of the resulting water had either soaked into the ground, filled the area's lakes, or added to the thick humidity. Yesterday, light rains had rinsed the winter dirt and grime into the lawns and fields. Then the clouds had vanished and the sun had come out to do the final drying, bringing the temperature up to almost eighty. Everything glowed, as if freshly polished and lit by a spotlight. The leaves were vibrant shades of green, the plowed fields were heavy in rich browns, and the sky was the blue of a deep, clear, mountain lake.

In the streams, ditches, and lakes around

1

Greenwell, a record crop of mosquitoes had just hatched, but the people of Greenwell didn't care. They were all smiles at the beautiful day that proclaimed winter gone. They had shed their heavy coats for shortsleeve shirts, their long pants for shorts, their stocking caps for baseball hats. Everyone greeted one another cheerfully, the problems of the long, cold months forgotten.

Around Greenwell, spring was not only a time of the year, it was an attitude.

Candice and Ernie White both had the "attitude" real bad. Candice was a solidly built twenty-five-year-old–woman, big boned as they say, with wide, red cheeks and bright, blue eyes. She wore a shortsleeved cotton dress and sandals. Having heard that the weather forecast the night before said it was to be clear and beautiful in the morning, she had spent the entire evening painting her toenails pink. Bright pink.

While Candice's large frame seemed to dwarf everyone she met, Ernie was the opposite. He looked as if a strong wind might lift him away at any moment. He too was just barely twenty-five, and quickly going bald. Since he was a good five inches shorter than Candice, she was always rubbing the top of his head, like she was patting a dog. He hated it, but never said anything. Not many people said anything to Candice.

Yet Ernie loved her as much as anyone could love Candice. He hoped that they would have kids someday, as soon as they had a little more money saved up. Candice said she wanted kids, too, but never seemed to really want to talk about it.

Since just after an early breakfast, Candice had been humming, a smile glued to her lips as she worked. Ernie found himself whistling softly. Candice hated his whistling, said it was never in tune, but today he didn't care. It was spring and he would damn well whistle if he wanted—especially if she wasn't around.

It was more than just the weather that made them both so happy. They were the owners of Flowers and Such, a small florist shop and greenhouse tucked away on the northern edge of Greenwell. Spring had finally arrived, and it had had the good taste and timing to do so on a Saturday, perfect for their business.

The main shop of Flowers and Such was the size of a large bedroom, with a glass cooler to keep the cut stock as fresh as possible taking up a good deal of the floor space. Running the length of the back wall was a counter, which held a cash register and racks of greeting cards. There was also a back room for stock and flower arrangements, and beyond that a glass and wooden greenhouse forty long paces in length and twenty steps wide. It was the biggest greenhouse within fifty miles and Candice and Ernie were proud of it.

They had been preparing for this day for months, stocking up on bedding flowers, shrubs, and small trees, getting ready for the spring planting that the people of Greenwell would suddenly feel like doing, now that the weather had turned.

Their little greenhouse was packed almost solid, with only small paths left to walk on between the merchandise. The smells of the various flowers mingled, forming an overwhelming aroma. It was almost as if twenty different bottles of perfume had been spilled on the front counter of a department store. Candice loved it. Ernie didn't notice.

When the day dawned clear and beautiful, Ernie had taken a bunch of the shrubs and potted plants out of the greenhouse, arranging them in front of the store so the customers could see them. At five-before-nine in the morning, Candice had flipped the sign on the door to "Open." They were almost ready and, if all went well, it would be their busiest day of the year.

It might have been, too, if they hadn't run into a little problem with some alien visitors.

"Candice?" Ernie's voice broke the peaceful morning quiet. "Can you come here for a moment?"

Candice wiped her hands on her apron and headed through the back room and out to the greenhouse. Normally she would have complained about Ernie just calling her, as if she had nothing better to do but run to his side every time he wanted her. But the morning was too nice for anything so petty to ruin her mood, so she just kept humming as she came through the door and into the humid air of the greenhouse, letting all the wonderful smells cover her.

Ernie said, "Over here."

The side door of the greenhouse was open and

Ernie was standing just outside in the sun, looking puzzled.

Candice joined him.

Beside the greenhouse were two flowering plum trees. Both were about ten feet tall, with extra-thick trunks, each one bigger around than one of Candice's upper arms. Their roots looked as if they had been balled up and the dirt shaken out of them. Both trees had pink and purple flowers that covered their tops, almost like hats.

"When did you order these?" Candice asked, moving to inspect the limbs of one tree. "They're beautiful."

"Didn't order them," Ernie said. "And I wouldn't have left them out here if I had."

"Pretty trees, anyway," Candice said. "Different than any flowering plums I've ever seen. Thicker trunks. A lot more branches. We should be able to get at least a hundred bucks for each, don't you think?"

"Yeah," Ernie said, frowning as he looked the two trees over. "But we didn't order them."

Candice only shrugged. "Driver from Thompson's Delivery must have left them here when we got in that last order of shrubs. If we can sell them, we'll pay him for them. If not, he can have them back—no skin off our nose."

Ernie nodded, not really liking the idea, but knowing it wasn't possible to argue with Candice.

"Move them out front," Candice said, "beside the window, one on each side. I'll make the price tags. You think a hundred and twenty-five is too much?"

"Better stick with ninety-nine ninety-five," Ernie said. "We want to sell them, don't we?"

Candice frowned, then nodded. "I guess you're right. But they sure are pretty trees. Different."

"That they are," Ernie said.

At that moment the world changed for Candice and Ernie. In the four years that they had owned Flowers and Such, they had never seen a plant move. At least, not until today.

Now they were both smart young people. And Candice even read the *Planet* every week. But she had never believed in aliens. She read the tabloid mostly for the diet articles, ignoring all the "silly" stuff. However, she should have paid more attention to the alien articles, because the two flowering plum trees outside their greenhouse were, in fact, aliens. Actually an alien couple named Cistena and Autropur. They were members of the Zahurians, a race of plants who resembled *prunus americana*, the flowering plum tree.

But there were a few differences between the American flowering plum tree and a Zahurian. Cistena and Autropur were highly intelligent, could fly an interstellar spaceship, and loved meat. Any kind of meat. None of that could be said for your average flowering plum tree.

Cistena, Autropur and 206 of their closest friends had come to Earth, ready to spread out their roots for a year-long picnic on humans, dogs, cats, deer, even other aliens. They would eat just about anything that didn't have roots. Around the galaxy, they were a hated race, for obvious reasons.

So, as Candice and Ernie watched, mouths open in shock, the two flowering plum trees moved.

First, a branch from Autropur, the tree on the right, reached out and encircled Candice's neck like a green necklace, yanking her forward into its leaves and flowers.

"Gack!" she said. Since Autropur had her by the throat, that was the best she could manage.

Ernie stood still, looking extremely surprised, as Candice fought the flowering plum tree.

Then Cistena, the other tree, snapped out a low limb that suddenly seemed five times longer than it had a moment before. The branch easily cut off both of Ernie's legs below the knees, flipping him onto his back in the dirt with a heavy thud.

Blood spurted everywhere.

Candice again tried to scream, but the moment she opened her mouth, a branch filled it, curling down her throat, reaching for her insides.

She gagged, her eyes wide with panic, as the limb down her throat got a grip on something and retracted, pulling her stomach and throat upward. With a gurgle, she passed out, slumping into the outstretched branches of the tree. They held her up. Autropur had really strong branches, capable of holding up much more than Candice.

Down in the dirt, Ernie was struggling with Cistena, but was having even less luck. His blood spurted out of the stumps of his legs onto the ground. The thin branches of the tree were like steel wires, impossible to break or even bend too far. They covered his head, his waist, and wrapped around his chest, cutting into his skin in a hundred places.

Without even seeming to strain, the flowering plum tree picked Ernie up and slammed him against the ground. Candice had done that to him a few times, but never as hard as the tree was doing.

Once.

Twice.

Then over and over and over, as if Cistena were trying to punch a hole in the dirt with Ernie's body. Before too long there wasn't an unbroken bone left in the little man, which was just the way Cistena liked her humans.

The two plants piled the bodies between them, then, ten branches on each tree worked at once: cutting, slicing, dicing, faster than a human eye could follow.

Ten roots from each tree sucked up skin, muscle, bone, clothes, and anything else that had been attached to Ernie and Candice. Fifteen seconds later, the two plants had finished their meal.

On the right, Autropur spit out Ernie's belt buckle, fillings, and shirt buttons, using a root to dig a quick hole and bury them. Cistena spit Candice's toenails, fingernails, and earrings into the hole, then Autropur quickly filled it with dirt. With a few more sweeps of their roots, the blood on the ground was either sucked up or covered over.

They then went back to standing beside the greenhouse like two normal flowering plum trees.

Cistena shuddered in delight. Their ancestors had been right about this backward planet. There really was unlimited food.

Autropur burped, a low chirping that sounded a lot like a bird looking for its mate.

Cistena whipped out a branch and smacked his trunk in disgust, then the two went back to standing still, waiting for their next meal. Only a slight spring breeze moved their dark leaves and beautiful purple flowers.

Get your facts first, then you can distort 'em as you please.

—MARK TWAIN

The target range smelled of burnt wood and sweat. Smoke curled lazily from the remains of two targets fifty paces away from the firing line. A half dozen oval scorchmarks covered the far wall, indicating where the targets had been missed. Each of the ovals was the size of a dining room table.

Jay climbed slowly out of the padding against the back wall of the range, stretched a sore muscle in his shoulder, and took a deep, slow breath to make sure he hadn't broken a rib. He was sweating as heavily as a man sitting in a sauna. His white shirt was soaked and his black pants were ripped. He worked out every day, could run a crook or alien down in no time flat, and was stronger than most ex-New-York–cops, yet he was getting a workout simply firing this stupid

2

little gun. Actually, he was getting more than a workout. He was getting beat up. Every time he pulled the trigger it felt as if a bus pounded into his chest.

He held the tiny gun up to the light as if studying it might help. He knew exactly what it was and what it looked like. It was called a Noisy Cricket and was the size of a small kid's squirt gun. It weighed no more than two ounces, and looked positively ridiculous. He could carry one in his suitcoat pocket and it wouldn't even make a lump. Yet the little gun had the kick of a Central Park policeman's horse who's had its tail yanked.

Jay brushed the sweat from his eyes and squinted down the range. At least this time he had managed to hit the target. That was an improvement. With a normal gun he could have plugged three shots into a circle the size of a quarter from this distance, but a Cricket wasn't a normal gun. He had hit his target slightly off-center, blowing the head off a mock alien, but he had still ended up in the padding from the recoil.

He moved slowly up to the firing line, where his black jacket and tie were draped over a metal counter. There had to be a way to fire the Cricket without getting knocked on his butt. And if it took him a year, he was going to find that way. It had become a matter of pride. He punched in a new target. Another wooden alien dropped into place.

"Having fun?" a woman's voice said from the entrance to the range. He knew exactly who it was: Elle, his partner. She used to be Dr. Laurel Weaver,

New York City mortician, and a beautiful woman. She was still beautiful, but the identity of Dr. Weaver had vanished from all public records. Now she was known only as "L."

Before Jay had joined the Men in Black, he had been James Edwards, New York detective. Now he was just "J." Most of the time he didn't mind vanishing from his old life. Most of the time. Once in a while he wondered what he'd be doing if he'd remained a cop. But right now his biggest regret was that Kay had once handed him a Noisy Cricket.

Jay glanced up at Elle. He had thought he made the black suits that were the standard MiB uniform look good, but she made them look dynamite. Ever since Kay had retired, Jay and Elle had been partners. After nine months now, they were starting to get the hang of things at MiB, although in that time nothing had come along that was as exciting as that first case with Kay. Still, Jay and Elle had solved their share of problems for the planet Earth and the MiB. They were quickly gaining a reputation as more than just rookie agents. Jay liked that reputation.

"Havin' a blast," Jay said, answering her question while wiping the sweat off his brow with the tail of his white shirt.

"I can tell," Elle said, moving to stand beside Jay and eyeing the results of his practice. Then she glanced at the Noisy Cricket. "Didn't read the manual on that weapon, did you?"

Jay wasn't much for reading manuals. And lately that seemed to be all he'd been doing. There were at least a thousand different types of aliens in the known area of space and there was a manual on all of them. Just learning who was human and who was alien in New York alone had taken him months.

And besides learning about all the types of aliens, Jay had had to learn all the rules that governed the existence of these aliens on Earth, not to mention their weapons, their eating habits, and their sex lives. He had gotten to the manual on alien sex about a week before and had been so nauseated, he hadn't picked up another manual since.

But he wasn't about to tell his partner that it hadn't occurred to him to read the manual on this weapon. It was just a pistol with a nasty kick, after all. He'd been firing pistols most of his life.

Elle seemed to know he hadn't read the manual, though, possibly from the blank look on his face. She snatched the Noisy Cricket out of his hand. "Stand back and I'll show you how it's done, Tiger."

Jay stepped out of the way, quickly checking the pads behind Elle. He still remembered the first time he'd fired a Cricket inside that old jeweler's shop. He'd smashed an entire wall of hat hooks with his back, and the next shot had tossed him into a pile of garbage. At least she was going to end up with padding to cushion her fall.

"You fired a Cricket?" Jay asked, moving behind the counter and shaking his head, trying to keep from laughing.

"Nope," Elle said, placing her feet sideways to

her target, as if she were firing a bow and arrow. Her left shoulder was toward the target, even though she was right-handed.

"Read the manual, though?"

"Yup," Elle said, sticking out her right arm as if she were aiming the Cricket at Jay instead of down the range. Then she cocked her wrist, turning the Cricket so that it pointed at the target.

"Hang on now," Jay said.

"Why?" Elle asked. She used her index finger to point along the barrel of the tiny gun, like she was pointing at something in the distance and around a corner. The Cricket was a good two feet away from her body.

Jay had never seen anyone hold a gun like that before. She was going to be lucky not to break a wrist. And there was no way she could hit anything standing like that.

"Because," he said. "You—"

Too late.

Staring over her left shoulder at the target, she fired and the alien target exploded, spraying smoke and splinters. Elle stood her ground calmly for a moment, her hand still outstretched. Then she turned to Jay and tossed him the Cricket. "Good little purse weapon if you really, *really* don't like someone. Might have to get me one."

Jay glanced at the little weapon in his hands, then back at Elle, who was grinning. A sort of "who's the hotshot now?" grin. He'd seen it more times than he cared to admit over the last few months.

"Come on," she said, smoothing out her black suit jacket and heading for the door. "Zed needs us in his office as soon as possible."

"Why didn't you say so sooner?"

Elle almost snorted. "Because you seemed so determined to figure out that Cricket first. I might even have let you try a few more times if we didn't have a crisis on our hands."

Jay flipped the gun onto the counter and grabbed his coat and tie. Then, with only a quick glance at the remains of the target Elle had destroyed, he followed his partner, doing his best to ignore the aches in his back and shoulders from all those landings in the padding. As soon as he had time, he'd find the manual on alien guns and read it. Every damn word of it.

Zed's office was a glass and wood bubble, elevated above the main floor of the Immigration Center. Hundreds of aliens and humans filled the vast atrium below, going about their business.

To Jay, the place looked like a giant airport, with lines at the counters and everything. At the moment there were only about fifty aliens waiting to be processed into the city and out onto the planet. A slow day.

A massive flat screen filled one wall of the atrium, with two octopus-like aliens sitting in front of it. They were called the twins, since their real names were nothing a human tongue could handle. They each had eight arms which were always in motion over the controls in front of them. Their long eye-stalks jerked and stared at the big screen, apparently watching all of it, all at once. Jay knew from experience that those eyes did see just about everything that went on, which was why they were in charge of tracking the exact location of every alien on the planet, every moment of every day. They were very good at what they did.

Today they looked busy, as always.

The inside of Zed's office was very much like that of any corporate executive, circa 1979. There was a massive desk with a notepad in the middle, and chairs arranged in front of the desk. It didn't look much like the center of a vast, secret organization assigned the task of safeguarding the planet from aliens. And it certainly didn't look modern. But Zed seemed to like it, and since Zed was in charge, who was Jay to tell him to get a decorator?

By the time they had reached Zed's office, Jay had managed to get his coat back on and his shirt mostly tucked in. His tie was around his neck and he felt lucky to get it that far. He knew, without a doubt, that he had dirt and dust and sweat all over his face.

Zed raised an eyebrow at Jay's disheveled appearance, but didn't say a word. Instead he motioned for them both to be seated.

Elle dropped into the chair closest to Zed's desk while Jay eased his sore frame into one farther away, closer to the big window overlooking the center.

Zed's current secretary, Bartrick, stumbled into

the room with a hissing sound and placed a mug of something on Zed's desk. Bartrick was a Zadock, a race that moved at a snail's pace most of the time. It seemed Zed was constantly trying out new secretaries, but Jay had no idea why he'd even try a Zadock. It clearly must have been for some political reason.

Bartrick stumbled beside Zed's desk, but wasn't moving fast enough to fall down. Zed ignored him as the secretary slowly headed out of the office and closed the door.

With a flick of his wrist Zed activated a large holographic screen floating in the middle of the room above his desk. The screen was a large, detailed map showing the North American continent. On the map were four red blinking lights.

"Unauthorized landings," Zed said, nodding at the screen without really looking at it. "We're not sure why, who's doing it, or what they're dropping off. But we do know it's the same ship."

Jay knew that unauthorized alien landings were the most common and important thing MiB forces investigated. But usually a ship only touched down once—either staying or dropping something or someone off and then making a break for it. In the latter case they very seldom got far.

But the same ship coming in and out four times was very, very unusual.

"Same ship?" Elle asked. "How come the orbiting platforms haven't spotted it?"

"Don't know," Zed said, sounding annoyed.

"We're trying to figure that out. Maybe a new type of shield."

"Comin' down the seams," Jay said, staring at the evenly-spaced dots.

Zed looked at him with a frown. "You want to say that in English, Junior?"

"Even the best security networks have dead areas," Jay said. "Seams."

Zed nodded. He worked on his keypad for a moment, then looked up at Jay. "The twins are checking."

"Are there any other patterns?" Elle asked, staring at the screen.

Zed punched a key and small times and dates appeared by each dot. The first landing had been in Connecticut, the second in Michigan, the third in Minnesota, and the most recent in western North Dakota.

"Twenty four hours apart, almost exactly," Zed said.

Elle nodded. "And I'll bet they're almost the same distance apart. Right?"

Zed punched a few more keys on his desk. "Within a few miles."

"Floating seams," Jay said. "Someone found one of our weak links and is goin' for gold."

Zed only grunted and kept keying in numbers. A moment later a green dot appeared on the floating map in northern Idaho. "If they stay with this pattern, twenty hours from now there will be another landing."

"And you want us waiting with open arms?" Elle asked.

"Yep," Zed said.

Both Elle and Jay stood and headed for the door.

"And Junior," Zed added. "Have Elle show you how to use a Noisy Cricket before you hurt yourself."

"She already has," Jay said over his shoulder, trying to keep his voice even.

Zed nodded to Elle. "Good job."

"My pleasure," Elle said.

Bartrick stumbled into the open doorway beside Jay and stopped. Then he sort of snorted and moved into Zed's office past Elle.

Elle managed not to laugh—at least not until the door to Zed's office had closed behind them.

> *Once you remove the absurdity from human existence, there isn't much left.*
>
> —ALEXIS A. GILLILAND

Spring had come to northern Idaho. A few dirty snowdrifts still lined the main street of Pineville, but the bright sun was making short work of them. The grass on the county courthouse lawn had that new-green look, and Miller's grocery had rose bushes and other bedding plants displayed outside the front of the store, waiting to be bought.

Outside the little town, the spring run-off filled the river as the warm day baked the tall, pine-covered mountains. The air held the smell of pine and freshly mowed grass. Not a cloud marred the perfect blue of the sky.

"Doesn't look like this place has changed in thirty years," Elle said, making sure she kept the LTD under the posted speed limit of twenty.

3

Jay figured she was right on the money. Their black '86 Ford LTD looked almost modern as it cruised up the main street of Pineville. Most of the buildings dated from the forties and fifties and half of them needed paint after the long winter. Only the bank looked new enough to have been built in the seventies.

Jay stared at the few people out on Main Street at ten in the morning. Compared to New York, this place was as alien to him as some of the aliens they chased. There wasn't a business suit in sight, and no one seemed to be in a hurry. Pickup trucks were the vehicle of choice, and most of them had gun racks in the back windows and tool boxes in the beds. In his entire life, Jay had never ridden in a pickup truck with a gun rack, and didn't plan on doing so anytime in the near future.

A bumper sticker on the back of one truck they passed read, "The South lost the first Civil War. We'll win the second."

Elle glanced over at Jay, shaking her head in disgust.

"There weren't no brothers in Mayberry," Jay said.

"Lucky we don't have to stop for breakfast," Elle said.

As they passed the edge of town she kicked up the speed, effortlessly moving the LTD to sixty on the empty highway. Of course, the car could go much faster than that. It also had more weapons than most tanks. But from the outside, it just looked like a polished black Ford. As with many things in the MiB organization, their cars weren't quite what they appeared to be.

There were a bunch of houses along the road near town, and a small subdivision branching out along a river. But the farther they got from town, the farther the farms and homes in the narrow valley were spaced out on both sides of the highway.

Jay glanced down at the small tracking device in his lap. It looked like a regular laptop computer, but it was hooked into the MiB satellite system, and four MiB planes flying patterns above the area. Along with two other ground units spread out over a fifty-mile area, the device would track any unauthorized spaceship, shielded or not, landing within a fifty-mile radius. He figured they had about ten miles to go before they were in the center of that range, near the estimated next landing site.

Two more pickup trucks passed them, heading into Pineville. Jay watched them go. The sooner they finished this job and got back to the dirty, dangerous streets of New York, the happier Jay was going to be.

Jay and Elle rode in silence along the tree-lined highway, letting the LTD eat up the miles. Snow-capped mountains now lined the narrow valley, and along the driver's side a river tumbled over rocks, heading back toward Pineville. There were no more homes in this area, and the scene could easily have been on a picture postcard.

Jay rolled down the window, letting in the cool,

almost biting, air. The scent of pine trees and mountain river filled the LTD, clearing away some of his grogginess. They had taken a suborbital flight to the area, but it had still taken two hours to get this far west. After his battle with the Noisy Cricket he could have used some sleep. His body still wasn't totally adjusted to the thirty-seven hour Centaurian day.

Elle looked as if she were enjoying the drive, one hand on the wheel, her gaze taking in the sights. In the city he usually drove, but she was more used to driving in the country and Jay didn't much care. She seemed completely at ease, more so than Jay had seen her since they first teamed up. More than likely that was because there wasn't another human in sight. Elle pretty much hated live people. Jay was just happy that she tolerated him.

"You like it out here?" Jay asked.

Elle shrugged. "I couldn't live here," she said. "I'd go crazy without all the taxi horns and construction noise of the city. And there's nothing to do. No delis."

"Or dead bodies."

"Wouldn't miss those much. Don't miss them now."

"You don't?"

Elle shrugged. "Well, once in a while. They don't say stupid things and get in my way all the time." She glanced at him. "You miss being a detective?"

Jay looked out at the river. "At times."

Another mile went by in silence, then Jay said,

"How about visitin' out here? You know, feet up, bag of chips, watching the potatoes grow?"

Elle laughed, rolling down her window and letting in even more of the fresh, morning air. "Yeah, maybe," she said, taking a long, deep breath. The wind roughed up her hair and flipped up the collar on her black suit jacket. "Tough to get smells like this in the city."

"Glade Air Freshener," Jay said.

At that moment the tracking device on Jay's lap beeped once, twice, then began emitting a long steady sound like a dial tone.

"Got 'em," Jay said. "Shit. Comin' in five miles behind us. Quarter mile up a side valley."

Elle rolled up the window and spun the LTD effortlessly, for an instant going down the narrow, two-lane highway backward. Then she punched the accelerator, sending the LTD sliding until the wheels finally got enough traction to jump the Ford forward again. She powered the car into a bend in the highway at almost a hundred. The car took it like it was on a rail, never wavering toward the rushing river below them.

Jay kept his gaze locked on the tracking device, ignoring her driving. After he had ridden upside down in the Queens Midtown Tunnel with Kay, there was nothing Elle could do to scare him. Nothing at all. Besides, he'd read the manuals on the safety features of the LTDs. Not only were they powerful, but they were virtually indestructible. As long as he was belted in, he was safer than a baby in a crib, even if she dumped them in the river at 150 miles per hour.

Now Elle kept the speed above a hundred, even staying in her lane to make sure she didn't surprise some local driver coming the other way on a blind corner.

Two minutes and twenty seconds later Jay said, "Comin' up. Ship's a quarter mile up that-a-way." He pointed out the window at the mountains on his left. Why an alien ship would want to land here was beyond him. But many things aliens did were beyond him.

Ahead, along the river, were nothing but some scattered houses. Pineville was just a few miles down the valley.

Elle dropped the speed back under eighty and then yanked the car hard left, skidding the LTD sideways a short distance over the pavement before bouncing it through a small ditch and up a dirt road no wider than the car.

"Nice driving," Jay said. He hadn't even seen this road.

He braced himself with both hands on the dashboard while managing to stare at his tracking device and watch ahead at the same time.

"Someone's been up here recently," Elle said, pointing at tire marks cutting through the remains of a snowdrift. "Looks like a fairly large truck."

"Pickup time," Jay said.

"I wonder who's picking up what?" Elle said. "And who's delivering?"

Jay had a hunch they were about to find out. He

studied the tracking computer one last time. "We're gettin' close." He punched a button on the dashboard of the LTD that signaled to the backup that they were coming up on the target. About three miles behind them was a containment truck, and standing by in the air were two MiB silent-running helicopters which could be on site in minutes. That was one thing about most MiB missions that Jay liked. They always went after the bad guys with backup. Much better than most of his busts when he was a New York City detective.

Elle shoved the LTD hard up the dirt road. In places it was no more than two tracks through the brush, and small streams cut across it in dozens of places. The car slid sideways in the mud, but Elle recovered as Jay dumped the tracking device into the backseat.

He turned around again just in time to brace himself as Elle banged the car over a small ridge and through a stand of pine trees, digging the front end of the LTD into the dirt.

He pulled out his Series 4 De-Atomizer, a gun about ten times the size of a Noisy Cricket and as nasty in firepower. Kay had loved his Atomizer and Jay was learning to love his almost as much.

"There," Jay said, pointing through the trees.

Elle only nodded, focused on her driving.

Ahead of them was an alien ship about the size of a large moving van and just about the same shape. It was shimmering slightly, as if underwater.

"Shielded," Jay said, indicating the shimmering effect.

Beside the spaceship was a regular Earth delivery truck that said, "Frederick's Florist and Fine Plants" on the side.

"Shielding didn't do them any good this time," Elle said. She slammed the car into a slide, coming to a stop with Jay's door closer to the craft and the delivery truck.

"It's a Pseudolarix ship," Jay said. "Watch your ass."

Pseudolarix were big, dangerous aliens who would buy and sell anything for a price, including humans.

Elle nodded, drawing her gun from her suit-coat pocket before she even opened her door.

Jay stepped out, Atomizer in hand. Walking as if he were strolling up to a ticket counter on Times Square, he made his way around to the space between the ship and the truck. He had been right (score another one for the manuals). Three Pseudolarix were there, in the open hatch of the ship. Another one was in the back of the delivery truck, along with about twenty purple-flowered trees. There were still another twenty trees in the spaceship.

Near the door of the delivery van was a human, or an alien who looked like a human. Jay suspected the latter. Either way the guy froze, looking stunned.

Besides being just plain mean, Pseudolarix were the smugglers and pirates of this sector of space. They had absolutely no morals, from everything Jay had read and heard about them. But nothing had prepared him to come face to face with a Pseudo.

He stopped and stared up at the three in the ship. It was like staring at a herd of elephants. African elephants, to be exact. They stood ten feet tall on four legs, with crusty-looking gray scales instead of skin, and two small eyes on either side of a long trunk. On their trunks were a dozen tentacles that could pick up a pin and hold an Atomizer at the same time.

Jay remembered a briefing Zed had given him and Elle about Pseudos. Their thick legs could smash a car, their tails could rip down a tree and, from what Zed had said, a Pseudo's skin could stop a blast from an Atomizer. And it seemed they got very angry, very quickly.

The three facing him were all wearing some form of headphones, with wires extending down into their large ears. If they hadn't been so dangerous, Jay would have laughed at how ridiculous they looked.

"Okay, big guys," Jay said as casually as he could, his gun still at his side. "Drop the shrubbery and come out with your trunks up."

All three Pseudos in the spaceship looked at him for a moment, then one of them snorted, which Jay understood as a combination of "go to hell" and "eat bay leaves."

Then, moving as a unit, the three Pseudos in the spaceship and the one in the back of the delivery van charged him. Three of them grabbed Atomizers. Out of the corner of his eye Jay saw the human reach into the front seat of the van.

"Shit!" Jay raised his gun to fire at the mass of gray death rushing at him.

The ground seemed to shake like a San Francisco street. Jay got off one shot, aiming for the soft pink area just under the trunk—a place he remembered from Zed's briefing as being their weak spot.

Then, just as he was about to be trampled, he dove and rolled through some short brush beside the delivery truck, coming up on one knee, ready to fire again. The human had pulled out an Atomizer and was turning on Jay. Jay hit him square in the chest, smashing his body back inside the cab of the van.

One Pseudo's shot just missed Jay, charring a bush behind him as the alien raised its trunk and fired while running. Another shot and the front of the delivery van erupted in fire and exploding metal.

Elle fired from her position on the other side of the truck, cutting down the Pseudo that had been shooting at Jay.

Jay's first shot had taken down one of the big creatures just outside the ship, but that left two elephant-like Pseudolarix still standing, one armed.

"Give it up," Jay shouted.

Both Pseudos turned their backs on Jay and Elle and headed into the pine trees, crashing toward the river. Both Jay and Elle held their fire. Hitting a Pseudo in the ass with a shot from an Atomizer wouldn't hurt it, and would likely just make it angrier than it already was.

"Nice shot," Jay said to Elle as he checked the closest downed alien. The creature was more than dead. Elle's shot had gotten through the pink spot and scrambled its insides like a broken egg.

"You too," Elle said, glancing at the alien Jay had killed. It would never smuggle another shrub again. Jay quickly checked the remains of the apparent human in the cab. As he had suspected, it was a Biclite, the hired sidekicks of the Pseudos, and the only race that would work with them. From everything Jay had read, Biclites had the brains of a poodle, and acted like slaves around the Pseudos.

Jay moved back over to Elle. "Biclite in the cab."

She nodded and they stood, watching, as the two remaining Pseudos crashed down the hill through brush and trees, making more noise than a train as they made their getaway.

"I wonder where they think they're going?" Elle said, checking her gun and then heading for the car. "We've got their ship, and I doubt there's another one close by."

"What I want to know is why they were smugglin' trees," Jay said as he stared at the ten-foot–tall specimens in the van. "Dyin' for a shrub doesn't seem right by me."

"Who knows?" Elle said. "Come on. We can't let the Pseudos get into Pineville. It would be containment hell."

"Yeah," Jay said. "Rednecks and alien-elephants don't mix."

With one more quick look at the trees in the shimmering spaceship and the back of the delivery van, he shrugged and turned back to the car.

What the hell were the Pseudos up to? Jay shook his head as he climbed in beside Elle. Sometimes there was just no explaining aliens. Especially hard-to-kill ones that looked like African elephants and smuggled plants.

Basic research is what I am doing when I don't know what I am doing.

— WERNHER VON BRAUN

They met the containment truck on the highway after a wild ride down the dirt road. It took Elle's full concentration and driving skill to get off that mountainside. She loved driving outside the city, but it had been years since she'd been on something as primitive as this goat track. And she'd never driven on a muddy road with this much power at her fingertips. It was a matter of balance: power versus control. Twice she had slid off the trail, plowing through brush until she got back on track. And once she had simply mowed down a small six-foot pine tree. But in far less time than it had taken her to go up the road, she had them back on the pavement.

Beside her Jay let go of the dashboard and signaled that the containment crew should

4

stay close to them. Then he called in a backup team to hold the area around the ship. They were going to need containment around the two Pseudolarix trampling through the countryside more than around an alien ship on a mountaintop in the woods.

One of the backup choppers was already overhead, tracking the path of the runaway aliens, and a second was in position high over the abandoned spaceship.

"They're ahead of you a quarter mile," the spotters in the air said.

"Those suckers can move," Jay said.

Elle was just as surprised at how fast the Pseudolarix could run, considering their bulk. And they were heading non-stop for Pineville.

"I'll get ahead of them," Elle said as she kicked the LTD down the highway at about three times the legal speed of fifty-five. She figured they were lucky it was still fairly early in the day. She didn't pass one pickup along the way.

Within ten seconds they were past the two Pseudos. Half a mile farther, she spotted a slightly wider area in the road and slammed the car to a sliding stop, ending up with the car facing back toward the Pseudos on the shoulder of the highway.

"Nice," Jay said as they both piled out.

Elle noticed that to her left and behind them was a quiet subdivision along the river. Beyond that, Pineville was having a normal morning.

In front of them, in the direction of their fugitives, were nothing but open fields for almost three hundred yards on both sides of the road. It was a good place to make a stand. Two MiB agents against two elephant-sized Pseudolarix. Elle figured the aliens didn't stand a chance.

Jay flipped open the trunk and grabbed a nasty-looking rifle from a case anchored inside. It was the same Phaser rifle that Kay had handed to him on his second day on the job. The same rifle that had helped bring down a bug's spaceship. Jay called the gun "Beauty" and Elle had no doubt it would drop a charging Pseudolarix in its tracks.

She pulled her own favorite Phaser rifle from the trunk and Jay slammed it shut. Elle liked Phasers as much as Jay. She just hadn't gotten around to naming hers yet.

"Ready to kick some elephant butt?" Jay asked, flipping on Beauty's power source. It gave a high-pitched whine and then a soft click.

"Ready," Elle said, powering up her Phaser rifle. It also whined and then clicked, indicating that it was ready to fire. She could feel the faint humming through her fingers.

Jay went across the highway, the heels of his black shoes making clicking noises on the pavement.

Elle stayed on the side with the LTD, moving down through a shallow ditch and out into the recently-plowed field. The ground was soft, but not muddy. She moved casually, confidently, not as if she were about to meet two huge aliens head on.

From the other side of the field, the sounds of

brush crashing and trees snapping echoed through the valley. It seemed the smugglers thought they'd have a better chance of not being seen by staying in the brush. Elle laughed to herself, shaking her head. These two were real deep thinkers.

A little ways from the road a couple had emerged from one house, and a woman from another. They stood on their porches, watching Jay and Elle. They were about to get a real show.

Too bad they would never remember it.

Both Pseudos burst into the open fields at almost the same moment. One was on Jay's side of the highway, the other on hers.

"Halt!" she shouted. She knew for a fact it would make no difference, but she was obligated to try.

Without even slowing, the first running, elephant-sized alien brought up its trunk and fired its Atomizer at her.

She dove hard to the right and into a ditch. The shot went wide and high.

"You got her suit dirty," Jay said to the charging alien. "She ain't gonna be happy."

Damn right. She wasn't. She knelt, aiming her Phaser. The Pseudolarix on Jay's side of the road wasn't armed, but still showed no sign of slowing. The Pseudo on her side fired at her again, this time almost hitting the LTD. Now both of the Pseudos were halfway across the fields and would be on top of the two MiB agents in seconds.

"Enough of this shit," Elle said.

Both she and Jay fired at the same moment, and

both of their shots hit the armed smuggler at the same moment.

Now, one blast from a Phaser rifle can stop just about anything built by man or alien. Getting hit with two Phaser rifles at the same moment causes extreme damage.

The huge Pseudolarix exploded with a massive ker-thump, like a wet rag hitting a counter. Only much louder. Where the alien had been there was now only an expanding cloud of steam, rust-colored blood, and gray scales.

The explosion echoed off the mountains and was finally drowned in the sounds of the river.

Elle turned her rifle back on the remaining Pseudolarix as drops of blood and scales fell around and on her.

The other smuggler had stopped, looking stunned, as much as an elephant-like alien could look stunned. For a moment it stared in the direction of its blown-up partner.

"It be raining elephant in Idaho," Jay said.

Elle lowered her rifle and stood, brushing dirt and mud off her suit pants. "I hope this stuff washes out." She picked a piece of gray scale out of her hair and flicked it aside.

"Now," Jay said to the remaining Pseudolarix, who stood no more than fifty paces in front of him. "Surrender or become potato fertilizer. You call it, dumbo."

The smuggler raised its trunk and said, as best Elle could understand, "Eat clover."

"Personally, a good steak kicks it for me," Jay said. "But thanks."

Elle moved onto the road beside Jay and stood facing the alien.

The smuggler looked at Jay, then at Elle, then back to the spot where his partner had exploded. Then he looked at them again. "Eat bay leaves, human," it said.

"Clover," Jay said, correcting the alien. "I thought we were supposed to eat clover."

"Elephants have no memory," Elle said.

"Oh, yeah," Jay said. "Forgot."

The alien lowered its head, snorted like a mad bull, and then charged right at them, its feet spinning in the dirt as it churned for traction.

Elle brought her rifle up, holding it at her hip, and pointed it at the mass heading toward them.

"Was it something I said?" Jay asked as he raised his rifle and fired before the Pseudolarix could get within twenty paces. The blast from Jay's Phaser didn't explode the creature, but it had enough force to send the elephant-like alien flipping up into the air.

It landed on its back with a thud that shook the field and sprayed mud over the LTD.

"Shit," Elle said. "We just had that washed."

For a moment all four of the Pseudolarix's legs remained sticking straight up into the air, then slowly it toppled over and lay still.

"Should have given it up," Jay said, moving closer to the smuggler and making sure it was dead.

It clearly was.

"It couldn't," Elle said as she came to stand beside him. "For a Pseudolarix smuggler, being caught is a great dishonor. Being captured by a human would be even worse."

Jay frowned.

"Remember?" she said. "Zed went on about it in one of the briefings he gave us."

"Oh, yeah," Jay said.

Elle shook her head. She doubted he remembered.

Down the road a pickup slowed, pulling to a stop about a hundred feet from the dead Pseudolarix.

"More company," Elle said.

Jay waved and smiled at the stunned-looking man in the truck's cab. "I bet folks around here never saw a black man kill an elephant before."

The containment crew arrived within sixty seconds to clean up the mess and give the neighbors and the guy in the pickup new memories. None of them would remember an elephant firing a gun. And none of them would remember a man and woman in black suits stopping in the field. Even the tracks of the Pseudolarix in the brush would be removed.

Elle turned the LTD back onto the dirt road heading up to the ship. The backup containment crew was still a good three minutes away, so Jay and Elle were going to be first returning to the scene.

Elle let the LTD slide sideways in a patch of mud

and Jay shook his head as she floored it, getting the car up the dirt road faster than she had the first time.

One of the MiB choppers was hovering high over the landing area, making sure no one tampered with the craft. They had been gone less than fifteen minutes, but having an alien ship just sitting empty in the woods was something Elle didn't much like the thought of. And now that the Pseudolarix were dead, she couldn't place why it bothered her so much. Kind of like the feeling she had missed something in an autopsy. But over the years, she had learned to trust that instinct, and at the moment her instinct was telling her their mission wasn't over just yet.

Elle skidded the car to a stop in almost the exact same spot as she had the first time. Both the alien ship and the Frederick's Florist and Fine Plants delivery van were in the same place. She stared at the name on the van. Why were the Pseudos and their sidekicks, the Biclites, delivering trees? Where were they going with them? And who was paying?

Jay reached into the backseat and grabbed Beauty.

Elle nodded. He was right. They needed to be very careful. She pulled her Atomizer from her coat as she opened her door.

Jay got out and scanned the area, looking as worried as she was feeling. His instincts were clearly acting up, too. Not good.

Not good at all.

Jay followed the same path he had taken earlier

around the delivery truck, this time with his Phaser rifle charged and ready in his hand.

Elle went the other way, covering him. Around her the pine trees rustled slightly in the wind and in the distance the faint sound of the river echoed up through the canyon.

The two dead Pseudolarix were still in place. Good. And she could see one leg of the Biclite hanging out of the cab of the van. Also good.

The back of the spaceship was open as before, and the ship's shielding was still working, giving the skin of the ship a watery look. Great.

The back door of the delivery van was also still open. Fine.

But the cargo of purple trees had vanished into thin air, or so it seemed.

"Gone?" Elle said, standing with her hands on her hips and staring into the ship's open cargo door. She looked back at the florist's truck. "How the hell did that happen?"

"Good question," Jay said.

Her instincts were still screaming. She carefully checked the surrounding area. Nothing looked different. There was the alien ship, the delivery van, and a forest of pine trees around the small clearing. Far above them the MiB chopper hovered, silently watching the area.

Elle pointed up and Jay nodded. He reached into his coat and pulled out a phone. "Patch me through to the chopper over the landing site."

He waited a moment.

The area around them was so still that she could

hear the words "Airborne Three" come from the phone.

"This is Jay. Any vehicle movement in or out of this site since we left?"

"No, sir. Only you."

"Shit," Jay said, glancing at Elle and shaking his head.

She reached out and he handed her the phone. "Patch me through to Zed," she said.

There was a moment of silence, then Zed's voice came back clear. "Go ahead."

"Pseudolarix smugglers," she said. "All four dead, plus one Biclite."

"Good," Zed said. "Their cargo?"

"Trees," she said. "While we were chasing two of the smugglers, the cargo vanished."

"Shit," Zed said. "We've got meat-eaters." Then he muttered something about always being afraid this would happen someday.

"Did I miss a manual?" Elle asked.

Beside her Jay really looked puzzled.

Elle only shrugged, not knowing what to tell him yet.

"No," Zed said. "You didn't. What did those trees look like?"

"About eight to ten feet tall," Elle said, "with dark leaves, purple flowers, and thick trunks. They seemed to be sitting on balled up roots. I thought they were flowering plum trees."

"Shit," Zed said again.

Then nothing. It was as if the phone line had

been cut. After a moment Elle said, "Hey boss, *shit* ain't helping us here."

"Sorry," Zed said. "Just pulling up a deeply classified file."

Elle shuddered. The entire MiB organization was so classified that no government on the planet even knew it existed. Every day before lunch it learned, and kept, secrets that could destroy the planet. Elle didn't want to know what kind of problem would need special classification in the MiB system, but she was about to find out anyway.

"How many were there?" Zed asked.

"I'd guess there were about forty or so, total."

Zed sighed. "That means with five landings of the Pseudo smugglers, we're facing more than two hundred trees."

"Boss," Elle said. "Could you bring us up to speed here?"

"Yeah," Zed said. "Sorry. Get back in the car and I'll fax you the entire file."

From down the road the sound of a truck slipping in the mud broke the quiet. "Containment has arrived," Elle told Zed. "All right if they secure the site?"

"Yeah," Zed said. "As long as you can't see any of those purple trees."

"Not a one," Elle said, scanning the edge of the pine trees again, just to be sure.

"Then let the containment guys at it. But don't make another move until you read the file."

The phone clicked off and Elle handed it back to Jay.

"Well?" Jay asked.

Elle shrugged and turned toward the car as the containment truck roared into the clearing. "The big guy was making no sense. Something about meat-eating trees and a top secret file."

"Top secret?" Jay asked. "For MiB?"

"Yeah," Elle said. "Weird, huh?"

"Wow," Jay said. "I really don't think I want to know what that might be."

"We got no choice, good lookin'," Elle said. "We're getting the fax."

*If you would keep your secret from an enemy,
tell it not to a friend.*

—BENJAMIN FRANKLIN

Zed's comments about a top secret file had both-
ered Jay so much he didn't even want to roll
down the window while the file was coming
through to the LTD fax, even though the
temperature inside the Ford was over a hundred degrees. Elle must have felt the same
way, since she climbed in behind the wheel
and slammed her door, then set the air con-
ditioning to full blast.

The fax equipment was inside the dashboard panel of the LTD, hooked into a secure communications link to MiB
headquarters. The paper slot that fed the
faxes out was directly in front of the passenger seat. About thirty seconds after Elle and
Jay were back in their seats, a light on the
control panel blinked twice and the first
sheet of paper slid out of the dash.

5

"Classified: MiB Top Secret," were the only words on the paper.

Jay glanced at it, then handed it to Elle.

"Oh, this is going to be interesting," she said, putting the sheet facedown in the backseat.

"Woman, you thought dead bodies were interesting."

Elle ignored him.

The next sheet of paper clicked out and Elle scooted over beside Jay so they could read it at the same time.

The report gave details on the Zahurians, a race of sentient meat-eating plants. At full adult size, they stood about ten feet tall and looked startlingly like flowering plum trees with purple flowers, dark leaves, and thick trunks.

The Zahurians controlled an area of space that covered almost a hundred solar systems. On their home worlds they had a companion race of hummingbird-like servants called Melenas. The Melenas were smart birds, too small and too fast to eat, who served the flowering trees much like bees served plants on Earth. When away from home the Zahurians used a race called Biclites as errand runners and servants, the same aliens who often worked with Pseudolarix. It seemed there was a chemical in the Biclite blood that made the Zahurians sick, so they didn't eat the Biclites very often.

Due to an unusual climate, the Zahurians were able to raise just enough animals on their planets to feed them all, but not much extra. Their only dealings with other races was to raid them for food. It seemed they needed some variety in their diet to continue to produce offspring. Except for the Melenas and Biclites, they ate anything that moved and didn't have roots.

"Man-eating trees," Jay said, shaking his head as he took the next sheet out of the fax. "Galaxy's a screwed up place."

The next page detailed exactly how the Zahurians cut up and ate their victims. The lower branches of the trees were as sharp as razors and could extend four to five feet. Yet all of the tree's branches could be used to grasp its prey, and the trees were very, very strong. The Zahurians communicated telepathically and worked together to trap their victims. The two dozen exposed roots on each tree could suck up and dissolve anything, from human flesh to solid rock. The sap flowing through their limbs and trunks was green, acidic, and completely deadly.

Jay let Elle take that sheet for a closer look after he scanned it quickly. That was more information than he wanted at the moment, or maybe ever. He'd make sure he didn't get any of that green sap on him the next time he met the runaway trees.

More pages spewed out of the fax machine, detailing the Zahurian empire and how bloodthirsty the race was. There were only a few civilized cultures in the galaxy that dealt with them at all, and then only for large sums of money. Almost everyone else feared them enough to destroy their ships on sight if the Zahurians were caught out of their own territory.

"Explains the Pseudolarix doin' the drivin'," Jay said. "They'll take any chance if enough money is involved."

"Yeah," Elle said. "And I bet they felt pretty safe with the trees. It would be tough to eat something the size of an elephant."

"Good point," Jay said and went back to studying the file.

On the next page of the report Jay finally saw why this was classified information, even for MiB. It seemed that over the centuries Zahurians had been raiding Earth and several other civilized but backward planets. The report explained how Zahurian raids had probably caused the disappearance of the citizens of Machu Picchu in the Andes, the cliff-dwelling Anasazi of North America, and a dozen other human societies which had seemingly vanished without a trace. At the bottom, a study on the possibility of Zahurian influence on the disappearance of the dinosaurs was referenced.

"Shit," Jay muttered.

"They've been around a long time," Elle said.

He nodded. "Good diet."

The final sheet clicked out of the fax and Jay hesitated before taking it. Finally he picked up the report and held it out of the air conditioner draft so they could both read it at the same time.

The page described the reproduction patterns of the Zahurians, and how the Melenas were used to ease pollination. Jay thought back to the manual on alien sex and then quickly put it out of his mind. It seemed the Zahurians lived for twenty Earth years and sprouted a dozen or so offspring over those years if the food was Zahurian normal, meaning they fed on a large animal once or twice an Earth year.

The report theorized that on a planet with abundant food, such as Earth, two Zahurians could drop a dozen seedlings once a month. Those seedlings would grow to adulthood within one year and reproduce at the same rate. The resultant number of man-eating plum trees after ten years was more than Jay wanted to imagine.

The only good news was that Earth's atmosphere and weak yellow sun had a bad effect on Zahurian health. It seemed that after a few years on Earth, Zahurians slowly lost the desire, and then the ability, to move around. They would plant their roots into the ground and die from hunger within six months.

If they remained indefinitely on Earth, the Zahurian offspring would also plant their roots in the soil, eventually losing their taste for meat and switching over to sucking up water and nutrients from the soil like normal trees.

"That explains why they didn't eat us all centuries ago," Elle said.

The report ended with the supposition that the garden-variety flowering plum tree was a direct descendent of previous Zahurian invasions.

"Zed said there might be over two hundred hungry Zahurians spread across North America," Elle said as she flipped back to the beginning of the report and started to read it again. "What the hell are we going to do? We just let forty of them escape."

"Don't remind me," Jay said, staring at the pine trees and the mountains above them. He had thought the huge Pseudos were the threat, when it had been their cargo he should have been worrying about. That would teach him never to underestimate a situation like this again. It was one of the many reasons they were still called rookies.

Jay brought up the computer screen on the dash. A moment later Zed's face appeared. He was frowning. "Read the report?"

"Yeah," Jay said. "We both have."

"Good." Zed glanced down at the control panel on his desk. "I'm sending two more containment teams to your area. Use them as necessary to track down and kill every one of those meat-eaters."

"How about negotiating with them, boss?" Elle asked. "They might surrender."

Zed snorted. "You said you read the file."

"I did," Elle said.

Zed shook his head in disgust. "You can't talk to them. No language. You can't trust them, since they think of all animals as food. Not once in hundreds of thousands of years has negotiating worked with them. And each one, if let go, could kill and eat a thousand humans in a year. Understand?"

The screen went blank.

"Yes, sir," Jay said to the empty screen.

"The boss is a little short this morning," Elle said.

"Worried about becoming green sap," Jay said. "I don't much like the idea, either."

Elle looked at Jay. "Well, have you ever tracked anything?"

"A cab on 42nd Street," Jay said.

"I'm impressed."

"It got away."

Elle looked around at the forest and the mountains. "Wonderful. Just wonderful."

Plan: To bother about the best method of ac-
complishing an accidental result.

—AMBROSE BIERCE

The first three days since Cistena and Autropur had been dropped off in Greenwell, Connecticut had been good ones for the meat-eaters. Not only had they fed on the two humans who owned the greenhouse, they had also eaten an elderly human and her small, white-furred dog an hour later. The dog had been nothing but a snack, and the woman had been all skin and bones, yet to the Zahurians, it had been a feast. An entire year's worth of food at home.

And this was only on the first day.

In their briefing on the human planet, they had been warned about three things: spread out the killing, watch out for humans in black suits, and don't stay on the planet for more than one cycle of the planet around the sun. The third warning didn't concern

6

them, since they were scheduled to be picked up far sooner than that. And on their first day near the greenhouse at least fifty humans had gone in and out of the building, including two in blue uniforms who had searched the greenhouse, then closed and locked the doors. But no humans in black at all. Autropur had wanted to feed on the two in blue since they were plump, but Cistena had stopped him. As their briefing had said, they needed to spread out the killing of the humans. Three in this location was more than enough for one day.

In all there were 208 Zahurians on the excursion to Earth, and the same number of branches on a healthy adult. Zahurians often did things in groups of 208, considering it a blessed number.

Zahurians were also telepathic trees. They couldn't read other plants' or animals' thoughts, and for long distance communications, such as from a planet's surface to a ship in orbit, their thoughts had to be amplified. On the way in, the Pseudolarix ship had dropped two shielded amplifiers in low stationary orbits over this area of the planet. With a focused message, any Zahurian could thought-speak with any other Zahurian on Earth.

Zahurians always traveled in pairs. From their earliest memories, young Zahurians stayed with just one other tree. Zahurians were not sexual in the way animals are, but it did take two Zahurians to drop seedlings. The young trees usually met their lifelong mates during the early sprouting days in the growing centers, long before either had all 208 branches.

Cistena and Autropur knew that all the other Zahurians who had been dropped off in the first group had already eaten. The feelings of satisfaction and joy flowing through the cluttered thought waves were like a drug, making Cistena and Autropur giddy. Many of the second day's drop had also eaten, and even a few in the third wave. It was as if they had all found the fabled Holy Feeding Ground.

This entire planet was teeming with animals, big and small. When they returned to Zahuria, Cistena was sure that Earth would be added to the list of top resort worlds. Decent weather and unlimited food. What more could any meat-eating tree ask for?

Autropur wasn't so sure. The limitations on the length of their stay, plus the difficulty of hiring the Pseudolarix to get here made this trip very special. He doubted there would be another 208 coming soon. But he agreed with her happiness about being on Earth. They were very lucky.

On the first night, Cistena had decided they needed to get away from the greenhouse. Using the cover of darkness, they had pulled themselves down the side of a paved road. The slightly heavier gravity on Earth made it harder for their roots to lift and move them forward like they did at home. So they ended up having ten roots pull while ten roots pushed. The smaller roots kept them balanced. It was slower than they were used to, but it worked just fine. Just before sunrise they found a place to rest in an open field near other earth trees. They spent that day just sunning themselves, striving to absorb the weak rays of the yellow star. It was no wonder they had to limit the time of their stay to a single planetary cycle of the sun. Cistena knew that after only a part of a year, she was going to hunger for real light again. But still, she was happy.

That day they had eaten only lightly, snacking on an earth dog and a few flying morsels. But it was still more than either of them would normally have ingested back on Zahuria.

The next night they moved again, this time finding positions near a large human gathering place made of wood with a pointed roof. The area to one side of the structure was filled with earth trees and carved stones. Again they stood with other earth trees, blending in, covering their exposed roots by tucking them under low shrubs.

Both Cistena and Autropur were surprised that there were a few Earth trees nearby that looked like thin Zahurians, but after an hour of trying, Autropur couldn't get a thought out of any of them and gave up in disgust.

That third day they only snacked on the flying creatures. They stayed that night in the same location, resting, digesting.

It wasn't until the morning of the fourth day that everything changed. First off, two humans with a large machine rumbled into the open area near the two Zahurians. The humans quickly dug a deep hole in the earth, set up strange-looking structures over and near the hole, and then left. A short time later almost fifty humans walked slowly out to the hole carrying a large box. And almost all of them were wearing black.

Exactly what they had been warned to avoid.

Autropur almost had to force Cistena to stand still. Escape! Avoid humans in black. Escape! she thought desperately.

Autropur sent calming thoughts as Cistena's branches trembled. Stand still. Do not move. They do not know we are here.

Other Zahurian thoughts joined Autropur's thoughts, calming Cistena. After a moment Cistena's branches shook only slightly, as if a gentle breeze stirred them. But there was no other movement.

The humans in black stood around, speaking orally for a time, then lowered the box into the hole and left, leaving only the two men who had dug the hole behind.

A wave of relief filled their thoughts, as other Zahurians joined in. Why had they been warned of humans in black? There had been many of them very close to Autropur and Cistena and nothing had happened. Had that been a false warning?

Maybe humans who wore black and stood around a hole were without power? They had been warned that humans did many odd things. This hole-gathering ceremony was clearly one such event.

One of the two remaining humans stood in the shade near Cistena while the other worked near the hole, stacking things. She snaked out a root and grabbed the closest human by the leg.

"Hey," he shouted, startled. He tried to struggle against the root, but Cistena held on easily. Humans were such a weak life form, it was amazing they had developed as far as they had.

"Hey, Charlie," the human shouted. "Help me here, would you?"

The human near the hole looked over, then shook his head and started toward the human Cistena was holding. When he got within range, Autropur snapped out two branches and cut off the man's right leg. Autropur picked up the leg with one branch and started hitting the human over the head with it. Red blood splattered everywhere.

At that moment Cistena wrapped a dozen more branches around her prey and pulled him under her, slicing and dicing the meat into small chunks, easily sucked into her roots. The human stuggled for only a moment, then went still as she stuck one root into his head and slurped out the wonderful-tasting gray matter.

Autropur stopping hitting the other human with its own leg and started cutting the man up from the bottom, sucking in the pieces as he went. Within two minutes, there wasn't a sign that there had even been a struggle under the trees.

Hours later, Cistena and Autropur were both relaxing, enjoying the wonderful feeling of dissolving animal fat in their systems, when the bad news came in from the fifth and final drop of their traveling companions. Humans in black suits had interrupted the drop, had killed two of the Pseudolarix, and confiscated their spaceship—the only ship the Zahurians had to get home. Two Zahurians had managed to get a message out on the Pseudolarix communication link before fleeing, but they weren't sure any Zahurian ships had heard it.

Being trapped on the planet for the rest of her growth cycle frightened Cistena. What would happen to them after one cycle of the sun had passed, as they had been warned about? Others feared the same. Waves of thought-panic swept over all 208 of the Zahurians.

Autropur only burped, the noise coming from one root and scaring off a few flying creatures.

Keeping the range of her thoughts down so only Autropur could understand her, she focused on him and was surprised at what she felt.

Autropur was happy. He was thinking of how he would have no duties and unlimited food for the rest of his time. He was as content and pleased as Cistena had ever felt him.

Cistena listened to the panic from her other traveling companions flooding the thought waves, then settled down on her roots, blocking the thoughts so that she could relax in the sun. Autropur was right. They had come here as a treat and an adventure. Now they would drop seedlings, eat to their sap's content, and live until their bark turned black with age. Who cared what happened after one cycle? They would figure out what to do then.

Earth. Paradise. There were far worse places to be.

Wearing black, patent-leather shoes, a black suit, and a black tie was just fine for New York City, but not for climbing through Idaho forests on a hot spring day.

"We've got to talk to Zed about black tennis shoes as part of this uniform," Elle said, easing herself over a log and making sure her slick-bottomed shoe was secure in the snow before putting her weight on it.

"Already did," Jay said. "Months ago. Hated the idea."

"Too bad," Elle said as she slipped. She caught herself before she fell.

Jay stood behind her, shaking his head. He could climb through windows, run down a subway, and scale fire escapes faster than any cop in New York. But tracking a bunch of runaway trees through an Idaho forest wasn't on his list of top one thousand things to do. Not even close.

"This is stupid," Jay said, sitting on the fallen tree and swinging his legs over. On the other side, he slid for a few feet in the wet snow before he regained his balance. He was carrying Beauty, but he had the power set low and had been using it more for balance than anything else.

"So what do we do?" Elle asked.

Jay glanced up the trail they had just slipped down. The Pseudolarix ship and MiB containment crew were still visible through the trees. It had seemed like forever, but they hadn't gone two city blocks yet. In slick shoes, it was amazing they had gotten even this far. It was clear that they weren't going to catch anything like this.

The path the escaped Zahurians had taken was clear. It seemed they moved by dragging themselves along on their roots. Forty or so of them, in soft dirt and snow, left a trail wider than most roads and scored deeply into the ground. It was an easy trail to follow. With the proper footwear.

Jay and Elle had ordered containment crews to set up blockades along the road in the valley. There was no way of knowing how fast the trees could move, and someone had to follow the trail to see when, and if, the trees split up, and where they went. Elle had decided that "someone" should be them.

Jay glanced back at Elle, then pulled out his phone. "Three?" Jay said, addressing the chopper still holding position high over the Pseudos' ship.

"Containment Three. Go ahead."

"Drop two pairs of hiking boots to our location. Size fourteen wide and—" he glanced at Elle.

"Eight narrow," she said.

"—eight narrow," Jay repeated into the phone. "Also, bring us a forest-service ranger."

"Ranger?" the voice from Containment Three asked.

"Yeah," Jay said. "You know the big green building outside Pineville? Go there and bring us someone who knows these forests. And be quick, my man."

Jay flipped the phone closed and pointed down the hill along the trail the plants had taken. There was an opening a hundred paces ahead in the trees, wide and flat enough for a chopper to land. They would wait there until help arrived.

Elle nodded and smiled. "Race ya."

"On our butts," Jay said.

"It would be easier than walking," Elle said.

They ended up barely making it to the meadow by the time the chopper dropped in carrying their boots and a female forest-service ranger.

Jay and Elle both sat silently on a log, putting on their boots while the forest ranger stepped slowly away from the idling chopper. She looked stunned.

Elle got her new boots on first and stood, testing them as if she were in a shoe store. "Surprisingly good," she said, stomping around without slipping.

"Fashionable," Jay said, nodding at Elle's brown hiking boots under the black suit pants.

Jay tested his, also surprised at the snug fit. He'd been wearing nothing but the patent-leather dress shoes for awhile now, and he'd forgotten how good other shoes could feel. It really made him miss his tennis shoes.

Elle moved over to the ranger and extended her hand. "Thanks for coming."

"Didn't have much of a choice," the ranger said, shaking Elle's hand.

As Jay tossed their shoes back in the chopper and

waved it off, Elle asked the ranger, "What did they tell you?"

"That Federal agents needed immediate help. Nothing more. And trust me, I asked."

"Well," Elle said, "I'm agent Hellen Paterson, and that's agent Jayson Richards." Those were the two names Elle normally gave to strangers. Jay liked to do what Kay had done to him: give a different name every time. Elle hated it, which, he had to admit, was why he did it.

"Bonnie Ann White," the ranger said. She was in her late twenties, with short brown hair and deep brown eyes. She seemed to be in great shape under the green slacks and brownish Forest Service uniform shirt.

As Jay moved a little closer, the ranger pointed at the Phaser slung over his shoulder like a deer rifle. "That rifle is not federal issue."

"Experimental," Jay said.

"Yeah," Bonnie said, almost snorting. "Like the silent helicopter, right?"

"Ranger Rick with attitude," Jay muttered. "Wonderful."

"Remember we need her help," Elle said.

"Can you track shit?" Jay asked, pointing at the trail the Zahurians had made near one side of the open area.

"If I step in it," Bonnie said.

Elle laughed as Bonnie took ten long strides and stood over the Zahurian trail. After a moment she turned back to Elle. "You want to tell me what made those marks? They're nothing I've ever seen before."

"You'll see soon enough," Elle said. "But I can tell you they were made by about forty creatures. We need to make sure none of them break off and leave the main group."

Bonnie nodded. "Should be easy enough, from the looks of it." Without another word she turned and headed downhill along the trail, taking sure strides in the snow and mud.

"Hang on there a minute," Elle said as she and Jay scrambled after her. "There's one more thing you need to know about what we're tracking."

Ranger Bonnie turned to face the two agents. "Yeah?"

"They eat people." Jay tapped the Phaser rifle on his shoulder and smiled. He managed not to laugh at the way her tanned face suddenly went pale.

If everything you know is wrong, then so are the scary parts, so relax.

— SPIDER ROBINSON

The day was almost hot. There was still patches of snow on the ground around Jay, Elle, and Bonnie, but only in the shade under the pine trees. To Jay, it seemed like a summer day. He wanted, more than anything, to take off his jacket. But he didn't.

The three tree hunters had followed the trail of the forty or so Zahurians for almost a mile down the hill toward the main road and the river.

But Jay and Elle hadn't found any of the meat-eating trees and the containment crews along the highway hadn't fared any better. From what Bonnie could tell, none of the main group had left the others.

"They've got to be close," Elle said nervously. She now had her Atomizer in her hand. When she'd drawn the gun from her

7

jacket, Bonnie had raised an eyebrow, but she hadn't said a word. Jay liked that about her. Tough, smart, and except for the early remarks, almost silent. Too bad she wasn't going to remember any of this. The stories she could tell around the campfire . . .

Jay was in the lead when things finally changed. He was moving solidly but carefully through the pine, alternately watching his step and studying the shrubs and brush ahead of and beside them.

"Some of them broke off here," Bonnie said suddenly stopping. She walked down the main trail a few steps. "I'd say about a fourth of what-ever-they-are split off."

"Shit," Jay said, staring at the second trail that headed south toward Pineville.

"Is it possible," Elle asked the ranger, "to get all the way to Pineville along the sides of this mountain?"

Bonnie nodded. "Some steep areas a mile or so downriver, and a few nasty creeks, but sure."

"Farms between here and there?" Jay asked.

Bonnie nodded. "There's about a mile of farmers' fields and orchards closer in that they'd have to cross to actually get in to Pineville."

Jay just shook his head at the impossibility of the task. Somehow, in the middle of a national forest, they had to find forty specific trees. And quickly, before the trees started killing potato farmers and rednecks.

"You know," Bonnie said, "it might help if you told me what we're tracking."

Jay glanced at Elle and shrugged.

"Trees," Elle said.

"Trees?" Bonnie looked puzzled.

"Better to wait until we find one," Elle said. "Then you'll believe me."

Bonnie laughed. "Trees, huh? And I bet they're dragging themselves along by their roots?"

"Exactly," Jay said. "You catch on pretty quick for a forest ranger." He moved away from her, still trying to decide how to handle the ten trees that had split off from the pack.

Bonnie started to say something, then saw that the two agents were very serious. She shut up.

Loosening his tie, Jay moved to a low branch of a nearby pine tree and hung the tie to mark the start of the new trail. Then he pointed down the main trail. "We go after the bigger group first."

Elle nodded and started off.

Bonnie hesitated, glanced at Jay, then followed her, with Jay right behind her. After about ten steps Bonnie broke the silence. "Mind if I ask what these trees look like?"

"Know what a flowering plum tree in spring bloom looks like?" Elle asked.

"Yeah," Bonnie said.

Neither Jay or Elle said anything more.

"Oh," Bonnie said a moment later. For the next ten minutes they moved through the forest in silence.

Finally Bonnie stopped them again. "Looks like about half of the rest of them broke off here." She pointed to where the scraping in the dirt split into two paths again.

"Where's that go?" Elle asked, looking at the right fork.

"Straight down over a ridge to the highway and river," Bonnie said.

"And that way?" Jay asked, turning to the left.

"North, up the river," Bonnie said. "Looks like you got three groups. One headed downriver, one up, and one right toward it."

Elle pulled her phone out and flipped it open. "Containment North? Spread out up the mountain on the road side. A group is headed your way."

Elle closed the phone and turned to Bonnie. "Can you tell which group is the largest?"

Bonnie walked about ten steps downhill, then did the same along the side of the hill, staring intently at both trails. "More went straight down," she said finally.

Jay nodded. "Thanks. How far to the highway?"

"Not far," Bonnie said. "I'm surprised we can't hear the traffic from here."

"We've got it blocked," Elle said.

"Wow," Bonnie said softly. "There are going to be some pissed-off people."

"Better pissed-off than dead," Jay said. He clicked on the power for Beauty. The Phaser rifle's high-pitched whine filled the trees, ending with a click. Then he started down the hill, alongside the Zahurian trail.

A hundred paces later Bonnie said, "Ahead of you."

Jay froze, holding the rifle at chest height. The Zahurians didn't use conventional weapons, but the report had said their branches and roots could whip out over ten feet with deadly force.

Bonnie came up beside him and pointed down the hill. It took him a moment to see what she was pointing at. In some deep brush about thirty paces ahead were some purple-flowered trees, apparently hiding. It looked as if there were two of them.

Jay fired.

The brush, the Zahurians, and two pine trees exploded into smoke and dust. The sound echoed through the forest, fading after a moment to be replaced by the faint sounds of the river below them.

"Holy shit!" Bonnie said, staring at the damage Jay had done with the rifle. "Powerful gun."

They started moving slowly down the trail again, checking both sides until they neared the place where Jay's shot had blown a hole in the underbrush. There wasn't much left. Just parts of two Zahurians. A few of the branches were twisting and jerking, but it was clear these two were no longer a threat.

"They're moving," Bonnie said, more to herself than Jay or Elle.

"That's what we said." Jay stared at the severed limbs, then at what was left of the green sap, dripping off the remaining leaves and scattered in small dots on the ground.

"Don't touch the green sap," he said. "Acid."

Elle nodded. "Good thing you vaporized most of it. We need to remember that."

Jay could only agree. The last thing they needed was to shoot a tree to keep it from eating people and have the green sap destroy everything it sprayed on—including them. The ultimate final meal for the meat-eater.

"But—" Bonnie stuttered helplessly, her eyes wide.

Elle just patted Bonnie's shoulder. "Hang on now. We still need your help."

Bonnie closed her mouth and nodded, but she was clearly shaken.

The trail beyond the explosion point went over a small ridge and sharply down toward the river. Jay swung wide of the destruction, staying in the open space under the pine trees and avoiding any chance of touching the sap. He inched forward to look over the ridge. He felt more like Davy Crockett hunting bear than a MiB agent tracking aliens. How the hell did he ever end up in this job, anyhow?

The river was suddenly very loud, and about halfway down the hillside below him, Jay could see about twenty Zahurians moving through thick brush toward the highway. Their purple flowers were like shaking pom-poms.

He motioned for Bonnie and Elle to join him.

"Count them," Elle said, her gaze taking in the group of mobile purple trees. "We have to make sure we get every damn one of them."

"You're going to kill them?" Bonnie asked. "Why?"

Jay finished counting. "Twenty." He turned and

faced the forest ranger. "To them we taste like chicken."

"Twenty," Elle said.

"Agreed," Jay said.

"You mean you weren't kidding when you said they eat people?"

"For snacks," Jay said.

"Nasty creatures, really," Elle said.

Jay figured at the speed the Zahurians were moving, they would reach the road in less than a minute. He flipped open his phone. "Center containment, twenty meat-eaters trapped against the highway. We'll need clean-up. Others hold positions."

He pocketed the phone, then raised his rifle, switching it to wide beam. On that setting the Phaser rifle was like a flame thrower, except that the flame was invisible and so hot it simply melted almost everything it touched within a hundred yards. Jay had seen one turn a car into a smoking puddle in a sustained 30–second burst.

With a sweeping motion he burned the entire area where the twenty Zahurians were moving toward the road.

The brush around the aliens instantly caught fire and disintegrated. As for the Zahurians, their leaves were the first to go, then their flowers, then finally their branches. The latter turned black and crumbled to dust, their green sap boiling away as steam.

Jay flicked off the Phaser and studied the smoking hillside. It had been easy. Almost too easy. He knew, without a doubt, that the rest would not be so simple.

"Twenty-two down," Elle said.

"Need some marshmallows," Jay said, as he looked at the flames.

Bonnie only stood there, staring open-mouthed at the smoking brush where twenty moving trees had been.

In the church graveyard in Connecticut, Cistena and Autropur stood silently, digesting the two humans who had been assigned to fill in the hole after the strange ceremony. Other people had come from the building and finished the job the two had started.

Still later, other humans in blue uniforms had come to look around the area, but Cistena and Autropur had remained still, not taking another meal. Even Autropur was starting to understand that they didn't need to rush their feeding. There was going to be plenty for them for cycles to come.

Now, in the early evening, only flat brown earth remained where the hole had been, surrounded by the green lawn and odd stones. Not even the flying snacks hung around.

Cistena was in a good mood, even though some of the panic about their ship being taken was still flowing through the thoughts of the others. However, most of them had come to the same realization that she and Autropur had arrived at. If they had to be stuck, why not be stuck in paradise? Except for a weak sun, this was the perfect planet to raise young saplings and spend the rest of their lives in peace. Maybe someone from the home world would come for them after a few cycles. Maybe not. What did it really matter?

Suddenly a blackness overwhelmed her thoughts. Deep blackness combined with a searing heat.

She shuddered, her leaves moving as if a stiff breeze had blown through them. Almost instantly she snapped down her mental guard, closing off the waves of despair.

She knew what had happened. The humans in black had just killed two of their party.

She directed a tight thought at Autropur, who usually rested with his mental shield up, asking if he knew.

He did.

They stood silently, staring out over the green area and the filled-in hole. Suddenly, to Cistena, this planet wasn't such a paradise.

She slowly opened herself back up to the waves of thought pouring in from the other 204 members of her group. It seemed that twenty others were in danger from the humans wearing black, but they were moving away from the death scene as quickly as they could.

Cistena shuddered again. The sacred number had been broken. Nothing good would come of that. It never did.

Another wave of heat, anger, and then blackness filled Cistena's thoughts as the twenty in danger also died at the hands of the humans wearing black.

Once more she snapped down her defenses, but not before she caught the last dying images of her traveling companions.

Humans in black.

Weapons of heat.

Danger.

Earlier the beautiful evening had her believing that they were stranded in paradise. Now, as she looked out at the stones and the open field, all she saw was evil. Evil, and a place where the humans in black had gathered. How could they stay here?

The strongest image that had come through from her dead friends was of an evil human, dressed in black, standing on a hill with a big weapon, burning them as if they were so much animal dung.

She focused a tight thought at Autropur. They were supposed to eat humans, not be killed by them.

Prey didn't kill Zahurians. Zahurians killed their prey.

How could this be happening?

So we don't try to eat humans in black, was all Autropur would say. And we get away from this place where they meet as soon as darkness comes.

Cistena's leaves shook with a faint rustle. It was no wonder this planet was not a regular stop for Zahurians. It was a nightmare world.

He had only one eye, and the popular preju-
dice runs in favor of two.

—CHARLES DICKENS

It had taken Jay, Elle, and Bonnie an hour to backtrack and follow the group of Zahurians going north, up the valley. There were ten of them and they had split up into five pairs. The containment crews burned two pairs near the highway while Jay and Elle, with Bonnie's help, got the other three pairs hiding in the brush. None of the Zahurians had tried to fight back in any way, but Jay knew that wouldn't be the case much longer. These aliens were strong, smart, and had green acid for blood. So far they had been surprised, but that was over now. Jay was sure the war was about to start.

By the time they had finished off the second group, it was almost dark and the group heading for Pineville was still on the loose. But there was no way Jay was going

8

to keep tracking man-eating trees in the dark. He could think of simpler ways of getting killed.

They spent the night in MiB shelters set up near the Pseudolarix ship. When Bonnie had seen the spaceship and the remaining body of the Pseudo the containment crew hadn't finished with, she had turned to Elle with a stunned look.

"Who are you people?" she had demanded.

Elle had smiled and said, "We like to think of ourselves as public defenders."

The next morning, at first light, the three of them had gotten back on the trail of the third group. Jay had picked his tie off the tree and stuffed it into his pocket, since he had a new one on. He figured there was no point in letting a good tie go to waste.

They had followed the trail for a mile, through some of the roughest terrain Jay had ever seen. How the trees had managed to drag themselves over those streams and along those rock ledges was beyond him. But he had figured that where a meat-eating tree could go, he could follow. And he had been right.

The trees had kept going during the night. By noon, the trail was skirting along the edge of the forest, along some farmer's fields about a half mile from Pineville. Just a quarter of a mile up the road was where they had stood down the two Pseudolarix.

"Oh, oh," Bonnie said, studying the ground in front of her.

Jay followed her gaze. After following these trails for two days now, he was getting pretty good at understanding what he was seeing. From what he could tell, the trees had split up into five pairs, like the other group had done the day before. Five different trails headed off across the open field, all going in the general direction of Pineville.

"We've got problems," Elle said, staring at the small town in the distance.

Bonnie laughed. "You think walking plants are a problem, try spending time in that town."

Elle shot her with a puzzled look.

Jay said, "Oh?"

"Half the town hates anyone with color in their skin," Bonnie said. "And the other half thinks women should be slaves. You two are going to fit in real well."

"You live here, don't ya?" Jay asked.

"Heavens no," Bonnie said, seeming almost insulted by the idea. "Just stationed here. I'm from Los Angeles. I'll take LA over Pineville any day."

"Wonderful," Elle said. "Maybe we should let the Zahurians have the place."

"Zed would be pissed."

"Oh, yeah," Elle said. "Bummer."

Two hours later, Jay knew their concern had been on the money. All five trails ended on different streets on the edge of the small town. Two went into the subdivision near the river, and three skirted the edges of the town proper.

Now they had three choices. He and Elle could go climbing through people's yards, looking at their trees. That sounded like a sure way to get shot by some redneck with a hunting rifle. Not a good idea at all.

His second thought was to call two agents who would fit in better, but from the sound of Zed's update when Jay reported in this morning, all agents were out tracking trees from the other landing sites, just like they were doing here. So no "correct-looking" agents would be available.

That left the third choice. They had to get the locals to help them.

Jay figured that the best way to handle that task was with a show of force to the local constabulary. He put his Phaser rifle back in the trunk. Then, with Elle in the passenger seat and Bonnie in the back, he pulled the LTD up in front of the sheriff's office. Both he and Elle had changed back into their black shoes and put on new coats. Elle wanted them looking sharp while they were in town.

Coming to a hard stop behind the LTD was one of the larger containment trucks. On the side of the truck Jay had had them put the official-looking sign: DEPARTMENT OF AGRICULTURE.

Leaving Bonnie with the containment crew, Jay and Elle went into the sheriff's office, Ray-Bans in place.

The office smelled of sweat and cleaning fluid. A locked glass case of rifles stood against one wall and three desks filled the main area. Down a hallway at the back were a half-dozen cells—a couple with residents. The sheriff had a glass-walled private office on the right.

There were three deputies in the main room and all three stood when Jay and Elle entered. One even put his hand on his holster. All three looked angry. What a way to welcome guests to their town.

The sheriff was a tall, thin man who wore a baseball cap and had his uniform shirt buttoned up tight under his chin. He came to the door of his office, staring at them. He too, wasn't happy with what he was seeing. To him, Jay and Elle looked like trouble.

Jay had his flashy-thing in his hand. Actually, what he called a "flashy-thing" was a neuralyzer, given to the MiB organization by a friendly alien race. The size of a bloated pen, it could be used to erase and reset human memories. Jay had the one in his hand set for a two-minute erase and deep imprint of new information. He needed the sheriff and his boys to be very helpful in the coming hours.

Jay held up the neuralyzer and didn't say a word. He simply pointed at it. Having a black man come into their office was strange enough, but having him hold up a pen and point to it was really odd, so all the deputies and the sheriff stared.

The room was filled with a bright flash and the expressions of the sheriff and his men went blank, as if they were sitting in front of a television watching reruns of championship wrestling.

"Get started," Jay said to Elle. "I'll make sure no one is listening in the back. He went through the door to the cells and flashed the two men locked up back there, cleaning out their memories for the next five minutes. Then he quickly gave them memories of a beautiful, naked woman coming in to serve them lunch. They were prisoners, but they didn't have to suffer.

In the front, Elle had just finished telling the sheriff and his deputies what they were going to do to help the Department of Agriculture. She told the sheriff that he had been expecting their arrival and that the sheriff and the deputies were not to see them as a woman and a black man, but as very powerful people and nothing more. She told him that he and his deputies were to help Jay and Elle with everything they asked, because Jay and Elle were here to save Pineville from an agricultural disaster of terrible proportions.

Then Jay and Elle waited near the front door for the effects of the neuralyzer to wear off. When they did, Jay stepped forward, smiling.

"Sheriff," he said in his loudest voice. "Been looking forward to meeting you. I'm Agent Mann, United States Department of Agriculture." Jay indicated Elle. "Agent Isolda."

"Been—been looking forward to your arrival," the sheriff said slowly.

"Got us a real problem," Jay said. "Yes we do. Agent Isolda, tell him about it."

Elle stepped forward. "We need your help scanning the area for a certain type of small tree."

The sheriff nodded, so Elle went on.

"You all know what a flowering plum tree looks like?"

All the deputies and the sheriff nodded again.

"Good," Elle said. "We need to locate every flowering plum tree in your town, starting with the subdivision near the river."

"Why?" the Sheriff asked.

"Disease," Jay said, using the word like a swear word. "Don't get within twenty feet of those trees, men. You catch it, body parts fall off."

The sheriff started to say something, but Jay held up his hand and went on.

"Fingers first." Jay lowered his little finger so that, to the deputies, it looked like it was missing. "Little finger, then up the hand, one finger at a time."

Jay bent his wrist, letting them imagine that his entire hand was gone. "The worst," Jay said, staring the sheriff right in the eye, "is when your little soldier hits the dirt."

All the deputies fidgeted, looking uncomfortable.

"So," Elle said, frowning at Jay. "Don't go near the trees. Just come back here and report their location to us."

"Twenty feet," Jay said. "No closer, or—wham, bam, thank-you mama—everything drops."

Every deputy nodded gravely.

"Now get going," Elle said. "Subdivision first. Report back as soon as you see a flowering plum tree. Understand? We'll take it from there."

"Let's go, boys," the sheriff said. "We got important work to do."

Each of them grabbed their hats, then stampeded out the side door and into their patrol cars.

Elle glanced at Jay. "Little soldiers?"

Jay slipped his sunglasses into his pocket and shrugged. "Considerin' the audience, what would you call 'em?"

Elle laughed. "Good point."

Never throw shit at an armed man.

— LARRY NIVEN

The sheriff returned to the station within half an hour. Jay, Elle, and Bonnie were on the sidewalk, standing near the containment truck with the big Department of Agriculture sign on the side. Elle was drinking water and trying to stay cool in the hot afternoon sun. The snowdrifts along the town's main road were now nothing more than piles of gravel and water. It wouldn't be long before the snow would all be baked away. Until today, Elle had had no idea that it could get so hot so high up in the mountains.

During the wait, Jay and Elle had spent some time talking with the containment agents. From the looks of how this was shaping up, the containment boys were going to have to cover just about every move they made in Pineville, and maybe flashy-

9

thing just about every person in this town as they went. Elle wanted to make sure they understood that.

When she wandered back to the truck, she had discovered that the crew with them at the moment was the senior unit of all the containment forces working this incursion. "JE" was their leader, but instead of calling him JayEe, the other two members of his unit called him Pro, since he used to be a golf professional before he joined MiB containment. Elle wanted to ask him how a golf professional got picked for MiB duty, but decided to do it some other time. It seemed very odd going from plaid pants to black suits.

The other two containment agents were "KB" and "RL." Pro said R'Elle was brilliant with computers and his nickname was "Partner." He could alter any computer system invented by man, and a few invented by aliens. He got the nickname when he bet on a football game with another MiB agent, against Pro. The other agent had called him "partner" and the nickname stuck—especially when Partner won.

K'Bee's nickname was "Captain." That came, Pro said, from reading too many *Star Trek* books during his time off. Elle didn't ask any more, and Pro didn't volunteer.

All three of them looked relaxed. When Jay asked Pro why, he said they had been working as a team for years and had seen just about everything. They had really liked Kay during his time with MiB and they had all been sad when he retired.

When the sheriff stopped his cruiser next to the truck, Jay patted Pro on the shoulder. "Stay on our ass," he said. "We gonna leave a string of messes."

"Right behind you," Pro said. "Just like always."

The sheriff piled out of his car almost before it had stopped completely, and came running up to Jay and Elle. "Found two of them," he said. "In Craig Hansen's backyard."

"Take us there," Jay said.

He signaled for Pro and the containment truck to follow, and within a few seconds Jay was behind the wheel of the LTD, Elle beside him and Bonnie in the back, following the sheriff's car into the subdivision near the river. As they drove Elle checked to make sure both their guns were charged and ready. She was taking no chances on this. They had been lucky with the first two groups of Zahurians. She doubted that luck would continue.

The homes by the river were cheap, and had mostly been built in the late seventies—all at once and all from the same basic plan. They each had a big picture window in front, shrubs beside the sidewalk, and two-car garages. Most needed paint badly, and a few had obvious roof problems.

The more Elle looked around, the more she realized that this wasn't a place where people with money lived. It was a subdivision, sure, but these were the homes of lower-income families, struggling to get by, with multiple kids, cars on blocks beside the garages, and broken toys left on the lawns. This was an Idaho ghetto, just as oppressive to its residents as a city ghetto. It had a different look, different people, but the same feel.

Two police cars were parked in front of one faded blue house. Two deputies were standing near the cars, looking worried. Jay, Elle, and Bonnie climbed out and went to meet them.

"Anything fallen off?" Jay asked.

Elle managed to keep a straight face—barely.

The deputies quickly shook their heads, their eyes wide.

"Good," Jay said. "Anyone home?"

"No, sir," the deputy said. "Craig works swing at the mill. His wife, Honey, is visiting her mother in Boise with the kids."

The look of surprise on Bonnie's face was priceless to Elle. Bonnie clearly knew this young deputy, and didn't much like him. Having him say "sir" to Jay must really have been out of character for him.

"Where are the trees?" Jay asked.

"Behind the house, near the back fence," the sheriff said. "Two of them."

"Great work, Sheriff," Elle said. "Have your men keep looking for the others. There should be two more in this subdivision. If you'll stay here with Ranger White until we destroy these trees, I'd appreciate it."

"No problem," the sheriff said. He signaled for the two deputies to get moving.

Elle pulled out her Atomizer and motioned for Jay to go around to the right of the house, past the car on blocks. She'd go to the left.

Around back, the place looked more like a weed

field than a yard. There was a rusted-out barbecue and a broken swing set, hinting at a time in the distant past when the yard had been used.

Elle scanned the back fence, but didn't see the trees. Either they had left the yard, or had moved up closer to the house than the sheriff had described.

As she eased around the side of the building, a branch whipped out inches from her face. They were close.

Almost too close.

She dove backward, rolling in the weeds as the branch snapped past her head.

She came up firing, catching the Zahurian in the lower trunk before the tree could advance.

The Atomizer exploded the thick wood, sending bark and green sap in all directions. She could hear the sizzle of the acid eating at the grass and the side of the house.

Elle fired again, this time into the closest branches, burning them to dust, making sure that no more corrosive sap escaped the heat.

On the far side of the yard, the other tree was near the corner of the house, right where Jay was heading. The Zahurians had been planning an ambush.

"Jay," Elle shouted, her voice echoing through the maze of homes. "It's a trap! Come to my side!"

There was no response. The tree that had grabbed for her was down, but still moving, leaking acid sap in a pool on the ground. Quickly, she took aim over the top of its twitching branches and fired at the tree near Jay's side of the house. Her shot caught it square in the trunk about head high. Branches flew everywhere and many of its leaves caught fire.

She brought her attention back to the tree closest to her. It was still alive and trying to reach her.

With three more rapid shots, she burned the tree to kindling and black ash, sweeping the ground to burn off as much of the green sap as possible.

Beside her Jay appeared, gun up and ready. "I was slowed down trying to get around a wrecked car," he said angrily.

Elle pointed at the injured Zahurian who had been waiting for him. "Lucky for you."

Jay and Elle aimed and fired simultaneously at the remaining tree. It vaporized in a ball of smoke and flame, leaving only a few withering, worm-like branches.

"They're settin' traps," Jay said. "Going to get ugly before it's done."

"Yeah," Elle said, staring at the holes the green acid sap was burning in the side of the blue house. She looked down at the black, smoking earth where the alien used to be. It could easily have killed her if she hadn't moved fast. This time she and Jay had been lucky, and they both knew it.

The deputies found the other two subdivision Zahurians hiding in the remains of a small apple orchard. Elle and Jay took care of them, standing at a distance and burning them down to nothing before any of their harmful sap could leak into the dirt. After that the search shifted to downtown Pineville: the businesses and the older homes closer to Main Street.

Two more aliens were found hiding alongside a garage in a musty alley. Pro, Partner, Captain and the other containment crew had their work cut out for them after Elle and Jay finished those two, since neighbors had watched from the windows of at least five nearby homes as the man and woman in black burned the two alien trees to ash.

Yet Elle knew that so far their luck was still holding. The Zahurians hadn't figured out a way to fight back yet, and they had not been able to inflict a lot of damage. She had no doubt they would.

At five in the evening, the deputies found two more of the flowering trees behind a barn on the edge of town. Those two actually tried to make a run for it, pulling themselves along on their roots as fast as a man could walk.

They didn't get far.

"Two left," Elle said as they climbed back into the LTD after leaving the remains of the two "runners" for the containment crew to clean up. Jay was driving and Bonnie was in the back. During the tree-hunting, she had gotten more and more quiet.

"Yeah, but where are they?" Jay asked in frustration.

"They might not have come into town after all," Bonnie suggested.

Elle glanced at the buildings around them. Down

the road two cars waited at a stop sign. The town wasn't even big enough to have a traffic light.

"No, I've got a feeling they're here," she said slowly.

Jay nodded. "Yeah, me too."

"So," Bonnie said, leaning forward so that she was more between them than in the backseat. "You ever going to tell me what you two really do? Besides kill trees, that is."

Jay looked at Elle. "Why not?"

Elle shrugged. There didn't seem to be a point, except to keep Bonnie content for a few hours more. But she turned around slightly anyway, so she could see Bonnie as Jay cruised the LTD slowly back toward the sheriff's office.

"We work for an organization called Men In Black Special Services," Elle said.

"Thus, the suits," Bonnie said.

"She be quick," Jay said.

Elle shot him a dirty look and went on. "Our job is to protect Earth from invading aliens and police the aliens that live here."

"Aliens live on earth?" Bonnie asked. "You mean, like those trees?"

"No alien trees are allowed here," Elle said.

"Don't know," Jay said. "Warren Christopher seems kinda wooden to me."

"He's a Pontaxian and you know it," Elle said.

"Yeah, then explain Shaq? Wooden and tall to boot."

Elle glared at Jay and decided to say nothing.

She'd gotten into a few of these conversations with him. They were usually fruitless.

"Too weird," Bonnie said. "You expect me to believe aliens are living on earth and we don't know about it?"

Jay laughed as he pulled the LTD to a stop in front of the sheriff's office. "I said the same thing."

"Thousands of them," Elle explained. "Actually it feels strange to be in a town like this and know there isn't an alien living here. *We* know where every one of them is."

"Except the Zahurians," Jay said.

"Yeah," Elle muttered. "Except them. But we'll eventually track them all down."

"Not before a lot of people die," Jay said.

Elle was afraid he was right.

That silenced Bonnie's questions. Elle sat, looking distractedly out the window and up Main Street. It took her a moment to understand what she was seeing, but when she did, she laughed.

She pulled out her phone. "Pro, we need you and a second containment unit right smack in the middle of town. Block off Main on both sides of the courthouse."

"What?" Jay's head snapped around to study the street in front of them.

"There," Bonnie said, seeing what Elle was seeing. She pointed out the two flowering plum trees standing on either side of the sidewalk leading up into the courthouse. They had hidden their roots in the shrubbery and had been standing there all day as Jay and Elle, the sheriff, the deputies, and the containment crews had come and gone from the area. A couple of really clever meat-eaters. Considering they were a race that controlled a hundred worlds and built interstellar spaceships, it was hardly surprising.

"Great place to hide," Jay said. "Right in plain sight."

"Tough to run, though," Elle said, pulling out her Atomizer and making sure it had a good charge. "Real tough."

> *The reward of a thing well done, is to have done it.*
>
> —RALPH WALDO EMERSON

One containment van pulled up on the other side of the courthouse and turned sideways, blocking both lanes of the street as Jay, Elle, and Bonnie got out of the LTD. A few horns blared, but one of the containment guys got out and flashed a badge. The horns stopped.

"I feel like I'm in a showdown in a bad western," Bonnie said, glancing from the two guns Jay and Elle held to the empty street.

Behind the LTD, the sheriff's car slid to a stop.

"Got the last two right there," Elle said, pointing at the two trees sitting in front of the courthouse.

"I'll be," the sheriff said. "Never noticed them there before now."

10

Jay didn't want to tell him that was because the trees had just moved there last night.

Pro and his crew pulled their containment truck up beside the LTD and signaled that they were ready.

Jay motioned for Elle to move up the sidewalk while he crossed into the street. If they could get clean shots from two sides, the containment boys would have less to clean up. And the quicker they got this over, the fewer people would have to have their memory erased.

Jay was twenty steps up the street, when the main door of the courthouse opened and two men came out, laughing and talking. One was dressed in a sports coat, the other in a white dress shirt and brown slacks. Both were in their late fifties and Jay guessed they were local attorneys, or maybe even judges.

"Go back!" Jay shouted, running forward. But he was too late.

Before the men could react, the two plants moved.

Each plant grabbed a lawyer. The two men were so surprised, they didn't even have time to struggle.

It didn't matter if the Zahurians were thinking escape or dinner. As either hostages or shields, those two men had a life expectancy of about five seconds if Jay and Elle didn't act quickly.

"Burn the trunks low," Elle shouted to him.

He dropped to one knee. As the tree on the left struggled with its prey, Jay aimed and fired a focused beam just above the shrubbery, holding the trigger down to sustain the energy, hoping to burn as much of the sap as possible. With luck, the man's foot wouldn't drop and be caught in the blast.

To his right, Elle, kneeling on the grass, did the same to the tree on the right.

Almost instantly, both trees were severed from their roots.

The man on the left managed to yank free and roll into the grass as the tree toppled over. The instant the man was out of the way Jay burnt the tree again, hard, all the way up its trunk.

The guy on the right wasn't so lucky. He fell sideways with the tree, landing on it in a missionary position, his face buried in its leaves.

Elle switched to burning off the top branches above the man's head, but the guy seemed either to be in shock, or completely locked up by the tree. In any case, he wasn't moving and the tree wasn't kicking him out of bed.

Finishing off the tree on the left while running up the courthouse sidewalk, Jay headed for the tree on the right.

Elle was also moving closer, firing at the tree when she had a clear shot at leaves or trunk. But there was no way of telling if the guy was getting covered in sap or not.

"Cover me," Jay shouted to Elle.

He ran straight to the fallen Zahurian, jumped over a small pool of green sap, reached into the sharp branches, and yanked on the lawyer's foot.

The alien must have been in shock from all the hits Elle had given it, because Jay managed to pull the lawyer out of the tree's grasp. He was so limp it was like dragging a dead body.

The instant Jay had the man free, Elle burnt the tree to a cinder, then swept the area of sap with the Phaser's heat.

Jay rolled the man over on the grass as Bonnie and the sheriff came running. The guy had cuts on his face and arms, but otherwise looked to be in one piece, which was a lot more than could be said for the two Zahurians. And he didn't seem to have gotten any of the sap on his skin. A few drops smoked on his jacket and Jay quickly stripped it off of him and tossed it to Elle to burn.

"Judge Lloyd," the other man said, bending over his friend. The guy that had escaped was scratched in a few places, and his shirt was ripped, but he seemed to be mostly unharmed. "Judge, can you hear me?"

The judge moaned and then opened his eyes, blinking. "What happened?"

"Good question," the other hostage said, glancing up at the sheriff. "What did happened?"

"Diseased trees," the sheriff answered, looking stern.

The man frowned. "What?"

The judge, on his back in the grass, also said, "What?"

"Diseased trees," the sheriff said again. "You got all your fingers?"

The judge raised his hands and looked, then nodded. The other man did the same.

"Thank god." The sheriff's voice was very relieved and serious.

The sun had just dipped below the horizon and the evening chill had closed in around Cistena and Autropur when the blackness touched Cistena's thoughts again. The last of their companions at the final drop point had been killed by the humans wearing black. Forty-two of the sacred 208 were gone, killed by the very prey they were here to eat.

Cistena hadn't felt so much fear since the first cycles after she and Autropur had left the seedling grounds. All she wanted to do now was go back into space, back to their home. She didn't care how much food there was here, it wasn't worth it.

But Autropur didn't agree. He was sad for those who had died, although he didn't much care that the sacred 208 had been broken. The two of them were a great distance from the point where their friends had died. Autropur focused a tight thought at Cistena. They looked very similar to other Earth trees, and if they were careful, there would be no way they could be found. Just be calm.

Those thoughts comforted Cistena.

Autropur also reminded her that not one of them from the first four drops had been killed. And all had fed more than once on humans. They had even seen a humans-in-black gathering and hadn't been killed.

That, too, made sense to her. Maybe they really were safer than she was imagining.

But Autropur reminded her they needed to be careful. And to be careful, they needed to relocate. They had killed in this location. It was time to move on.

With this, Cistena agreed.

So, as the darkness settled over them, the two Zahurians dragged themselves toward another stand of trees in the distance. It would take them most of the night to travel the distance, but to Cistena, it would be worth it.

And if it made Cistena happy, it made Autropur happy as well.

New York has always been an absurd city to live in but, in a perverse sense, this is one of its delights.

— JOHN CORRY

The sun had vanished behind the tops of the Idaho mountains, but it was still a good hour before sunset. The chill had returned to the air almost instantly the moment the sun had vanished. Jay wagered that the night would be cold enough to freeze all the water that had melted from snow during the day. Strange place, these high mountains. Even stranger weather.

"So," Bonnie said, standing beside the LTD. "How does a person go about joining your MiB organization?"

"Be in the wrong place," Jay said, "at the wrong time."

"What?" Bonnie asked.

Elle laughed. "Never mind him. Trust me, if there's a need for your skills, MiB is not bashful about asking."

"Yeah," Bonnie agreed. "I noticed that when those two in black suits came into my office and dragged me out."

Just then Pro came up to Jay and nodded. "Almost finished."

Jay slipped his hand into his jacket and pulled out his sunglasses.

Elle did the same.

With a quick movement, he held up the neuralyzer and flashed Bonnie. No point in waiting. She wasn't going to remember meeting them, let alone wanting to join MiB Special Services. She was going back to the world of knowing, without a doubt, that there were no aliens on Earth. Jay almost envied her.

Bonnie's expression transformed from a look of surprise to a dull blankness.

"All yours," Jay said to Pro.

"Give her good memories," Elle said. "She helped us a lot."

"Yeah," Jay said. "She wanted to join us, too."

"Maybe she will someday," Elle said.

"Foolish woman." Jay pointed at the car and Elle got in the passenger side, leaving Bonnie in the containment crew's capable hands.

Jay hadn't even asked what story they were giving these people. He didn't really care. He was just glad to be leaving the little Idaho town. He could think of a hundred different alien home worlds he'd rather visit before coming back here.

He eased the LTD into a u-turn and headed out of town, staying within the speed limit. A half hour later they had traveled back up the valley to the pick-up point.

Two hours later, they were in Zed's office in New York City. And Jay, for one, was damn glad to be home. In the City he felt right, as if he belonged. He'd be happy if he never had to leave the City again. Fat chance of that, but the thought made him happy anyway.

"Good work out there," Zed said as the two settled into chairs in front of his desk.

Through the windows of Zed's office, Jay could see that the huge Immigration Center was operating at its normal frenetic place. The twins were at the big board, and at least a hundred aliens were waiting in lines to be processed for one thing or another. He and Elle had just killed forty-two illegally-landed aliens, and here life went on as usual. There was something comforting about that.

"Thanks," Elle said, in response to Zed's compliment.

"Got any of the others yet?" Jay asked, yawning. It was almost one in the morning New York time, yet Zed showed no signs of slowing down. Jay, on the other hand, wanted nothing more than his bed and a good night's rest. Both he and Elle were past their normal thirty-seven hour day, as, most likely, Zed was too.

"None," Zed said, his tone disgusted. "Just the forty-two you killed. We figured they dumped forty-two at each site, since 208 is an important number to them, for some obscure reason."

"Any ideas on how to track them?" Elle asked.

"None," Zed said.

"Can't see the trees for the forest?" Jay said.

"Something like that," Zed said, frowning at Jay. "But I want to see how you two hot-shots do." A holographic map appeared above his desk with a red dot showing in Connecticut. "I'm sending you to the first landing site. Got two other agents up there I'm pulling for the North Dakota site."

"North Dakota?" Elle asked. "Isn't anyone out there?"

"Got three other teams there already," Zed said. "We're going to focus on that site, where the tracks are the freshest, and work our way east as we clean them up."

Jay wanted to kiss Zed on the forehead for not sending them back out west. One trip this decade was enough.

"We're basically a holding action, then?" Elle asked. "Doing what we can until help arrives?"

"More like cannon fodder," Zed said.

"Cute," Jay said. "We're gonna need containment teams."

"And a base of operations," Elle added.

"Same crews as in Idaho," Zed said. "They'll join you up there tomorrow afternoon. Already got a building rented for you. Maps, phones, communications center, computers, and other equipment will be in place. Oh, and one more thing." He glanced down at his desk for a moment, then went on. "The Zahurians in Idaho got off a message before fleeing. We're not sure if it got through or not."

"Great," Jay said. Now there was a chance of even more trees coming. That was all they needed.

"Don't worry about that, now. Get some rest, get back on schedule, and keep me posted."

With that Zed went back to studying a screen on his desk, dismissing the two agents.

Jay yawned all the way to his bed. He didn't much like the way the alarm sounded six hours later. Six hours just wasn't enough to last through thirty-seven hours of day. But it was going to have to.

The building MiB Special Services had rented for the Zahurian elimination operations was an old farm supply warehouse about five miles from the location of the Pseudolarix's first touchdown in rural Connecticut. It smelled of old hay and machine oil, but otherwise looked as if it would work just fine. Jay figured that very few of the trees were still close to the actual landing site, since they had most likely been trucked some distance away by the Biclite to begin with. And it had been five days since they were dropped off. But having a headquarters in the center of the area might save them some time.

The warehouse had other good points. It was hidden behind some trees, down in a shallow valley. There were no nosy neighbors who would be in constant need of memory wiping. Plus the place was big and already set up with bedrooms, a dining room, a kitchen complete with a cook, and a main planning area combined with the communications arena. As far as Jay was concerned, it was perfect.

Elle, on the other hand, was not pleased about the clear signs of rats. She was a New Yorker who worked with dead bodies, so Jay couldn't figure out how she could be afraid of a few rats.

She hadn't answered that question.

By ten in the morning they were standing in front of a huge map of Connecticut on a wall in what Elle had instantly called their "War Room." Pro and his containment teams would be arriving by late afternoon with all their equipment, so Jay figured the two of them would get started by coming up with a plan of attack.

"So, rat boy," Elle said, looking at the huge map. "Got any idea where we start looking for forty-two killer trees?"

Until she made that comment, Jay actually hadn't had any idea at all. But the word "killer" snapped his mind from Idaho forests and physically tracking the trees to city thinking. And even though they were up in Connecticut, he needed to think like a city cop to catch killers.

When he and Kay had tracked the bug on his first case, they had watched the morgues. On this case there wouldn't be any bodies, since there was nothing left of the Zahurians' victims. But there was another place they could start looking.

"Sure do," Jay said, smiling at Elle. He picked up the phone on the desk. It had the customary dead sound of a MiB secure line. "I need research," he said.

A moment later a voice sounded on the other end. "What can I get for you, Jay?"

"Missing person reports," Jay said. "All of them for the last five days, in a circumference of, say, two hundred miles from the landing site in Connecticut."

"Great thinking," Elle said.

"They'll start coming through shortly," the voice on the phone said and then the phone went back to its dead sound. Jay hung it up and turned to Elle, who was also smiling.

"Of course," she said. "They're going to leave a trail, aren't they? Just like they did in Idaho."

"Yup," Jay agreed.

"But you missed something." Elle picked up the phone. "I need research, please."

Jay frowned, trying to figure out what she was talking about. After a moment she said, "We also need the missing animal reports for the same area around the Connecticut landing sight."

"Bingo," Jay said. Of course. He had been thinking only of humans, but Zahurians would eat anything that had blood and moved.

"Let's hope we get a bingo," Elle said, hanging up the phone. "The more data points we get, the better the trail."

"I couldn't agree more."

At that moment, the fax beeped and paper started spitting out. Missing person reports.

Reports of lost cats and dogs.

Reports of stolen farm animals.

Two hours later the fax was still spitting out paper.

> *Facts do not cease to exist because they are ignored.*
>
> —ALDOUS HUXLEY

The killer flowering plum trees left trails of miss-ing bodies like the trails of slime behind a slug. Elle was amazed at how simple it was to follow them, once she and Jay figured out how to code all the information coming in. But it took them some stumbling around in the dark to figure out which method was the best.

First, instead of the normal-sized map in the war room, they had the map of the area around the first landing site blown up so that it filled an entire wall, top-to-bottom. Jay had to dig around to find boxes to stand on so that he could reach the upper edges.

While he put up the map, Elle spent an hour hunting down and killing every rat in the warehouse, or every one she could find, anyway. And she found a lot of them. Every

12

time one disappeared in a puff of black smoke, she felt better.

She came back shuddering, sweat dripping from her forehead, but smiling.

Jay just shook his head when he saw her. "You spent years crawling around inside dead folks," he said. "Why bother with rats?"

She shrugged. "Target practice. You want to try to hit one with a Cricket?"

He frowned but didn't say anything.

Elle could face down just about any alien known, including the bug she blew to pieces before she ever joined MiB Special Services. She just didn't like rats.

"Big map," she said, wiping the sweat from her eyes. She brushed her hair back into place while she looked at her partner's work.

"Big area," Jay said.

Elle studied the map. It covered an area two hundred by two hundred miles, or over forty thousand square miles. There were six hundred hamlets, towns, and small cities inside that area.

"Impossible," Jay said, slumping down into a chair and staring at the wall.

At that moment, Elle had to agree with him. Finding forty-two small trees in that much space seemed out of the question. She dropped down into a chair beside him.

For the next half hour they both just sat, depressed, thinking, while the fax kept spitting out paper.

Elle stared at the map, then looked at the pile of

data coming off the fax machine, then looked back at the map. Somehow, some way, there had to be a method of getting all the information onto the wall, in a way they could use.

"Impossible," Jay said again, shaking his head.

"Maybe . . ." Elle said, still alternating between the pile of information spewing from the fax and the forty thousand square miles of territory on the wall.

"You got an idea?" he asked.

"Not yet," she said.

Sometimes the job of defending the Earth from the scum of the galaxy just seemed overwhelming. This was one of those times. Too much information, too much area to cover, too few aliens to find.

"Impossible," Jay said again. It was becoming a mantra.

"Maybe . . ." Elle began again, smiling this time.

Jay looked over at her. "You got an idea, spit it out."

"A different color tack," Elle said, moving to the fax machine. The idea was coming together for her quickly.

"You want to finish the sentence?"

"For every missing person, pet, or farm animal," she said, holding up a handful of faxed reports. "A different color tack."

"Why not," Jay said, and grabbed a handful of reports himself. "Better than sittin'."

Red tack for humans, blue tack for pets, and green for farm animals. Logical and simple.

The air-conditioning almost kept up with them as they worked, reading a report, finding the area on the map, sticking the tack into the map at the last known location of the missing person or animal.

Hundreds of tacks later, Elle stood back, staring at it. No real patterns were emerging. This was just make work, and she knew it.

"This isn't getting us anywhere," she said.

Jay stopped. "Why?"

"Wrong information," she said.

Jay stared at the map, then shrugged.

"Days," Elle said suddenly.

"What?" Jay was already moving back to the chair to sit down.

"Days," Elle said again. "We code 'em by days."

Jay stopped, looking at all the tacks they had stuck in the map, then nodded and started pulling them out of the wall.

Elle went to work on the new color code.

Red for anything missing the first day, using the time on the report the person or pet was first suspected of being missing.

White for the second day.

Blue for the third.

Green for the fourth.

Orange for the fifth day.

"Bingo," Jay said two hours later as he stood back and stared at multicolored points on the map.

Elle had to agree. It really was a *bingo*. In almost fifteen places there were clear trails as the Zahurians fed each day and then moved. Red, white, blue, green, and orange. Little colored lines on the map showing exactly where the trees had gone. In a number of other places, all the colors appeared in one small area, showing that some pairs of trees hadn't even bothered to move their killing grounds.

"Smack me with a cab," Jay said, standing back. "It worked."

"Of course," Elle said. "I thought of it, didn't I?"

Jay only snorted.

"We've got to report this tracking method to Zed," Elle said. "It will help the other teams."

"All yours," Jay said.

Elle moved over to the communications panel. Zed would love this, though he'd never show it.

Jay walked clear to the other side of the large room and stood, trying to get the big picture—literally.

Elle quickly outlined what they had discovered for Zed and signed off. She came to stand next to Jay.

"Make the boss-man happy?"

"Zed?" Elle asked, then laughed. "He'll pass our idea on to the agents at the other landing sites. He seemed almost upset that we thought of it."

Jay laughed. "Mad he didn't come up with it. Means he likes it."

"Yeah," Elle said. Then she stood beside Jay and studied the map. From the looks of it, some sort of truck, like the one they had seen being loaded by the Biclite in Idaho, must have dropped off the trees every fifty miles or so along side roads, most likely the first night. Every red pin was near a fairly major road. More than likely the truck had dropped off its cargo, then headed for the next site the next night. It would be possible to drive from here to Idaho in four full days. She didn't want to do it, but it would be possible.

Elle counted red pins. Thirty-seven. That number could mean a lot of things. Maybe not all the meat-eaters had a meal that first day and some of them ate twice, since there were a few red pins close together.

Elle then counted trails and clusters. Twenty. There should be twenty-one. Maybe one pair of meat-eaters was outside the map's radius, or not eating much. She figured they would worry about that possibility later. At the moment, they were going to be very busy tracking and killing shrubbery.

The fax machine kicked into life again and they were fed three more missing person reports, plus another missing animal report. Jay quickly added the pins to the map, extending four clearly marked trails.

"These aliens aren't too bright, are they?" Elle asked, shaking her head.

"I'd bet that's what they think of us," Jay said.

Elle laughed. "Never underestimate your enemy."

"Or your food," Jay said.

Pro and his two containment crews arrived right on time. Jay gave them a half hour to stash their bags in their rooms before they headed out. It was almost three and the heat of the spring afternoon was intense. If they got started by three-thirty, they'd have enough time today to get to a large number of the meat-eaters before dark.

While they were waiting, Jay and Elle discussed the best way to tackle killing the trees. They needed to make sure that they burned them as quickly as possible. That way there was less chance of splashing the green sap on anything or anyone.

Last thing they needed was to burn some poor bystander with green acid.

"And we strike quick," Jay said, "at as many as we can get to fast."

"Like shopping at garage sales," Elle said.

Jay looked at her as if she had suddenly flipped.

She laughed. "When you're going garage sale shopping, you plan your route before you ever get in a car. My mother lived in Phoenix and I went with her a few times on Saturday mornings."

"Strategic garbage buying," Jay said. "An Olympic skill?"

"Possibly," Elle said.

"Plan away," Jay said, pointing at the map.

Elle started by picking the end of the trail closest to their location, then numbering the locations of the other trails of missing person and animal reports. By her best guess, they might find ten of the Zahurian pairs by sunset.

If they were lucky.

"Yeah, right," Jay said, when she told him that

number. "The way it went in Idaho, we'd be lucky to find four."

She hoped he was wrong.

At three-thirty in the afternoon, they rolled out of the warehouse in their LTD, with Pro and two containment trucks right behind them. She was driving. The hunt was on. And for the moment she remembered why she had become a MiB agent. They were defending the planet from the scum of the universe, saving human lives as they went.

It felt good.

Twenty minutes later they found the first pair of Zahurians standing near the entrance to a small park in the center of a small village. Their purple flowers were like beacons against the green lawn and gray oak trunks.

They torched the two alien meat-eaters as a sweating, long-haired poet was reading his verse to a bunch of blue-haired older women on benches nearby.

Jay had suggested they spray the green acid on the poet and make the world a better place.

Of course, she knew he was kidding. But from what Elle had heard, it was pretty bad poetry. When the two aliens went up in flames, the poet was going on about cooking for a lost girlfriend, about bathroom fixtures, and about slime on a pond. Elle figured they had put the Zahurians out of their misery. She'd want someone to kill her if she was stuck listening to poetry about toilets.

It is better to be a live coward than a dead coward.

—ROBERT BLOCH

The vibrant oranges and intense reds of the spring sunset filled the sky, as if a mad painter had thrown buckets of paint at a blue canvas. But Cistena wasn't paying attention to the beautiful world around their leaves and above their flowers. Instead she was focused telepathically on their traveling companions, those who had landed with them at the first Earth site. Now some of their group were being killed by the humans wearing black, and it took everything Cistena had not to panic.

Beside Cistena, in the grove of Earth trees, Autropur sighed, also paying attention to the slaughter going on around them. In all the years of the Zahurian history, there was no record of a race such as the humans turning on them. Humans were so primitive,

13

they didn't even believe that other races existed. Their travel organizers had told them Earth was teeming with easy-to-catch food. That information had been correct. Avoid the humans in black and there would be no problems. The Zahurians hadn't even bothered to bring weapons. No Zahurian took weapons on vacations.

Yet they needed them. The humans wearing black had killed all of their friends at the last landing site, and now they were killing Zahurians in the first group. Eight had died, burnt in a black mental wave of pain and surprise. Now, the sun was setting and the coming darkness would hide their movements. They would all be safe from the humans for the night, at least.

At least they all hoped that would be the case. Maybe the humans could find them in the darkness, too.

"How are they finding us?" Cistena asked, sending the question directly to Autropur. "Do they have instruments capable of following our thoughts?"

"Possible," Autropur thought back to his companion. "But not likely. They are not advanced enough."

"But then how?"

"Humans are primitive animals. You read that in our vacation brochures. They follow trails. It is clear we are all doing something to leave a trail they can follow."

Cistena kept her fear contained for a moment, going over what Autropur had just said. There was no way a Zahurian could lower itself to thinking at human levels. Cistena refused to even try. It would only have hurt. Finally Cistena focused another tight beam at Autropur. "I have no idea what it might be."

"Neither do I," Autropur replied. "But we will discover it in time."

"Assuming we are still alive," Cistena said.

Autropur shot back, "There is no need to panic. But soon we must find weapons to use against the humans."

"If only our Melenas were here," Cistena said. "Or a rescue ship would come for us."

"It is possible for both to occur, if the signal got out at the last drop."

"If only it were true," Cistena thought at Autropur.

"We must help it become true," he replied. With that Cistena felt Autropur open up his thoughts to a wider band, so that the others left from the first drop could hear them. "I have an idea," Autropur thought clearly to all the remaining Zahurians.

One hour later, at exactly the same moment, all thirty-four remaining Zahurians from the first drop thought a focused call for help into the sky, sending it with all their power. It was something that hadn't been done in centuries, but they had all been told of the possible range of such a thought.

They repeated the action one hour before sunrise, this time joined by the Zahurians at the other three remaining drop sites. One hundred and fifty-eight Zahurians, all focused on calling for help.

Cistena had no idea if the call would be heard, but at least they were doing something, and that made the panic lessen.

Between calls, Autropur had had them move deeper into the Earth forest, farther away from the human roads and buildings. By morning they were buried in brush and other trees, so deep that not even the reds, pinks, and oranges of the summer sunrise lit the area around them.

The next morning, long before the sun brightened the east side of the old warehouse, Elle and Jay met in the war room to plan the day's attack. "Planning their garbage shopping," Jay had called it. Elle hadn't had her first cup of coffee yet, and had only given him a dirty look in response to his comment. She had warned him a dozen times not to mess with her before her coffee, but for Jay, the greater the danger, the more fun it was.

The afternoon before they had managed to find and kill eight of the trees before darkness forced them to return to the warehouse. The early quitting time on the hunt and nothing to do had allowed Jay to get a decent amount of sleep, even though it meant going off their normal thirty-seven–hour day. It had helped. He was feeling better than he had in a week.

They both stared at the huge map, Elle sipping on her coffee. Their tracking method was going to work, and that, for some reason, worried him. It *should* work. But at the same time, Jay couldn't shake the feeling that something was going to go wrong. If their information on these meat-eating plum trees was right, they had been around a lot longer than humans. They could fly in space, build ships, and were feared by hundreds of other races. It shouldn't be so easy to kill them.

"You get the new faxes of missing animal and persons," Elle said. "I'll pull the tacks from the ones we got yesterday and see what's left."

Jay glanced at the board. "Don't pull them. Just replace them with black tacks. In case some of the tracks are confused by inaccurate reports."

"Good idea," Elle said.

Jay headed for the fax machine. It had a pile of paper in it. Dozens of pets, about ten farm animals, and three humans had gone missing in the last twenty hours in the area their map covered. And one new report for a person already missing for three days had also been added in. These trees had to be stopped, and stopped quickly. Too many people were dying.

They added a new color tack for the current day's crop of missing, extending a bunch of the lines and confusing some of the old ones. Then, at six in the morning, their route planned, they headed out into the darkness with Pro and his containment crews right behind them.

The first stop was fifty-eight miles from the warehouse. From the looks of the map, two of the trees had simply found a spot and not moved, killing three humans, six dogs, and five cats. How two trees could swallow that much flesh was beyond

Jay. But somehow, unless there was another pair of Zahurians with them, two trees had done just that.

It took them almost an hour to get there and another half hour, as the sun came up, to find the two aliens flanking the path up to the front door of a country club. They toasted them and left quickly. Pro and his crew only had to leave their trucks to sweep up the ash.

Jay and Elle spent the rest of the morning searching for the next pair, finally locating them along a driveway to a funeral home. Jay was glad no one was being buried that morning.

Twelve down, thirty to go. Still happening too easily, but Jay wasn't going to look the old gift horse in the mouth too much.

At the other three remaining Zahurian landing sites, the MiB agents were also having a great deal of luck with the new tracking system. The North Dakota landing site, with seven agents and six containment crews working the countryside, had only six trees left to find, then most of the agents would move east. Jay figured that if they were lucky, the other sites would be cleared soon, and he and Elle would have help by the end of the week. He had no doubt they were still going to need it.

By three in the afternoon they had found two more pairs of Zahurians. One pair was hiding just inside the edge of a small apple orchard, their flowers giving them away. The second pair tried the hostage routine, like the ones at the courthouse in Idaho, but Elle cut both aliens off at the trunk before a branch even touched the two elderly women out for a stroll.

Jay had told Pro to give the two women memories of a sex-filled afternoon, but Elle had vetoed that idea.

"You're no fun, woman," Jay had said.

She had only smiled and said, "You don't know that, now do you?"

Sixteen Zahurians down, twenty-six to go.

And that's where it stopped for the day. From three in the afternoon to dark, they didn't spot another purple-flowered alien, even though they searched exactly where they thought the trees should be.

An hour and a half after dark they arrived back at the warehouse, tired, hungry, frustrated, and hot.

A rat ran in front of the car when they parked the LTD. Elle didn't even seem to care and Jay didn't have enough energy left to kid her about it. It had been one of *those* days.

Twenty-six meat-eating trees remained hiding somewhere in forty thousand square miles of northeastern countryside. Jay doubted that tomorrow was going to be any easier.

> *One should always get even in some way, else the sore place will go on hurting.*
>
> — MARK TWAIN

The sunrise was more of a fading, starting at black, moving to gray, ending with light. Clouds covered the sky above the forest, and the air seemed almost unnaturally still. The deaths of her traveling companions had Cistena almost paralyzed with fear. The humans dressed in black had somehow found and killed almost every Zahurian at the next to last drop site, and many of those in the other two areas. Their group still had over half its members, but now their calls for help from outside the planet were getting weaker, because of their dwindling numbers and their distance from each other. Autropur had said that if their first or second call hadn't been heard, the calls never would be. They would be on their own. No help would be coming.

14

Cistena refused to believe that, and had blocked the negative thought. Help had to come. Nothing else would save them, and Cistena said so to Autropur.

Autropur didn't agree, saying they could avoid the humans, and live a long and happy life—if they could just discover what was allowing the humans to find them. The answer came just after sunrise, from one of the survivors at the second landing site.

"Don't eat!"

The thought was intense and almost painful in its power as it was relayed to all the remaining Zahurians. Cistena actually flinched, leaves and flowers rustling.

"Is it possible?" Cistena asked Autropur.

"It is." Autropur knew the truth of it instantly. The humans were tracking them by following their feeding patterns. It had been so simple, so primitive, that no Zahurian had seen it. Luckily, Autropur and Cistena hadn't eaten for two nights, simply remaining in hiding. Others had not been so smart, or so lucky.

"What do we do?" Cistena asked.

"We remain hidden," Autropur said.

"And hope for help?"

"Yes, that also," Autropur said.

"And if no help comes?"

"We find weapons and fight," Autropur said. "Or we remain hidden. It is a choice we will make when it is time."

Above the two aliens the sky brightened. The sun

climbed, slowly heating the air to a hot, sticky mass.

Three more houses and eighteen-year-old Jeremy Halpren would be done with his paper route. The sun was coming up as he spun his bike into the Hendersons' driveway and hit the front steps with the banded newspaper. The paper bounced once and stayed on the second step.

"Yes," he said to himself, thrusting one fist hard into the air in a sign of victory. He'd missed those steps the last three mornings, but this time he'd got it right. It was going to be a great day.

He kicked the bike into motion and headed up the street, pedaling hard. Two more houses, then home. He had baseball practice today after school and with luck he'd be playing shortstop in the next game. He'd had this paper route for five years. He was going to miss it when he left for college.

He was in front of old man Cronk's empty field when the tree root snaked out of nowhere, grabbing his bike and then his arm and yanking him to the side of the street.

"What?" He tumbled to the pavement, the sticky branch holding him like a vise.

Another root grabbed one of his legs and pulled him across the street, scraping his back and shoulder on the pavement. He was being pulled toward two strange-looking trees. This wasn't possible. Someone was playing a joke on him. He knew it.

But it wasn't funny. And it hurt. If he hurt his throwing arm he was going to be really mad.

"Let go!" he shouted, his words echoing off the homes and over the empty field. He twisted, trying to get away. "You're scraping my arm!"

The roots didn't let go, and before Jeremy knew it he was on his back near the sidewalk, looking up at the two trees. Both trees were moving, as if they could get up and walk around like a person.

"Not funny," he said. In all his life he'd never been so afraid. Yet he didn't dare show it. If this was a joke he'd be laughed out of school and off the team for being afraid of a stupid tree.

Suddenly one of the roots snapped out and cut off his right arm. His throwing arm.

Blood spurted.

He was too shocked to scream.

Another root cut off his left arm.

More blood, all over his pants, spilling into the street.

His blood.

Now he screamed, but the sound was cut short by a root filling his mouth, choking him.

Two branches picked up his two arms and held them in front of him. Almost as if his two hands were waving good-bye.

Again he tried to scream, but the root just went deeper into his throat.

A dozen more roots lashed out from the two trees, cutting small pieces off of him. The pain filled his mind, his every thought, as he struggled to get free.

But the two trees kept cutting and slicing him.

And after a few more long moments, Jeremy blacked out. For good.

The paper-boy killers were easy to find. The two Zahurians were standing in plain sight, along the edge of a road, their exposed roots covered by brush. The senior in high school's bike had been found that morning in the middle of the street when he didn't come home after his route. The police had taped off the area as a crime scene, and Jay and Elle had heard the report on their scanner, even before it was faxed to them by MiB research. The bike was just a hundred yards from the aliens.

As Jay and Elle climbed out of the LTD, the two Zahurians tried to make a run for it, pulling themselves along by their roots toward the trees.

In all his years as a cop and his time with MiB, Jay had never felt such pure anger. He wanted much more than death for those two aliens. He wanted to pluck their leaves one at a time, rip every petal off their flowers, strip the bark from their trunks, break their roots.

He was pissed.

The police tried to stop the two agents from entering the area near the crime scene. Jay ignored them. Elle flashed a badge and held the police back.

Jay moved to stand between the two fleeing paper-boy–eaters and the forest, blocking their escape. He had his Phaser rifle in his hand, but did not point it at them.

Both aliens started whipping out their branches, trying to reach him, but Jay stayed out of their range, holding the rifle at his hip. He had it set on wide beam, so that it again acted like a flame-thrower, firing invisible, extremely hot flames.

"Why?" he asked, knowing he wasn't going to get an answer. But he asked it anyway. "Why?"

One of the trees picked up a rock and flung it at Jay, missing high and right.

Jay didn't even flinch.

Elle appeared beside him, facing down the two aliens. "They won't answer. They don't consider us any more than food."

"I know," Jay said. But that didn't help his anger. These two scum trees had killed a kid who had been doing nothing but working to earn a few bucks. And maybe, if Jay had been just a little faster yesterday in their hunt, this kid would still be alive. That was making him mad, too.

One of the Zahurians tried to lunge at the two MiB agents, but both stepped back out of the reach of the tree's grasping roots.

"They're telepathic, right?" Jay asked, staring at the two trees. He had an idea, born from his anger, but maybe it would do some good. Save a life.

"Yeah," Elle said. "That's what the reports say."

"A message," Jay shouted at the trees, firing his Phaser rifle in a quick burst at the lower branches of the two aliens.

Both trees burst into flames.

Now the two aliens were much more concerned

about putting out the fire than they were about the two MiB agents.

"That's got to hurt," Elle said.

"That's the idea," Jay said. Then he shouted at the two aliens to make sure they heard him—if indeed they could hear. "Tell your friends. *No more humans.*"

He knew it would probably do no good. But it made him feel better.

The two aliens used their roots to beat out the flames in their leaves.

"No more humans!" Elle repeated. The fire in one of the trees had almost been put out, so Elle singed the tree again, sending the flames even higher into the branches.

"No more humans!" Jay shouted.

They stood in silence then, letting the two trees burn.

The Zahurians kept trying to put out their leaves, but Jay and Elle kept restarting the fire. Finally, after lighting them a good dozen times more, Jay nodded at Elle and they finished the job, reducing the two trees to nothing more than ash.

As Jay and Elle moved back to the road, Pro, Partner, and Captain stood beside their containment truck, applauding. The police looked extremely puzzled.

Jay didn't normally advocate torturing the enemy, and wasn't proud of his actions. But if it saved a human life, if it sent a message to the other Zahurians, it would be worth it. Even though it wouldn't bring back the paper boy.

Without a word, he and Elle climbed into the LTD and headed for the next possible Zahurian location, riding in silence. In the street behind them Pro put on his sunglasses and turned to the police, holding a neuralyzer in his hand.

Jay hoped the aliens had gotten the point. Because he was angry, he had a big weapon, and his job was to rid the Earth of alien scum. The Zahurians had proven themselves alien scum more than once over the last few days. This morning had been the final straw.

> *My life's dream has been a perpetual night-mare.*
>
> —VOLTAIRE

The beeping, insistent signal that a call was coming in woke Jay from a dream.

In the dream, he was in the middle of a huge banquet. He was trying to eat a salad, but the lettuce kept slapping his hand, knocking the fork away. Everyone around him munched on their salads without problem, but he couldn't get a bite, no matter what he tried to do. When he stuck his fork in the lettuce, it screamed in pain. At one point the cherry tomato, with help from three croutons, had tried to make a break for the rug, staining the white tablecloth with a trail of orange French dressing.

Ugly dream. One he would remember. And there was no telling where the dream might have gone if the call hadn't woken him. He didn't want to think about the vegetables with the main course. More than likely the potato would have eaten the steak before he could get to it.

He rolled over, rubbed his eyes, and glanced at the glowing numbers on the clock beside his bed. Four in the morning. "Shit."

He punched a key on the computer beside the clock, then turned on his side to face the thing. After thirty-seven hours awake, he'd only been sleeping for three. That wasn't enough.

It flickered once, then Zed's face filled the screen. As always, he was dressed in his suit and didn't even look tired. The man must work on a seventy-four hour day. Or more likely he *never* slept.

"Slap some coffee into that bloodstream and wake up agent Elle and the containment crews," Zed said, "I'll fill you all in from your war room. We've got a skimmer."

"Skimmer?" Jay said, trying to clear the fog and the remains of the salad dream from his mind. A skimmer was an alien ship that came in low, but never touched down. Why would it be important that he know about a skimmer in the middle of the night?

"Zahurian skimmer," Zed said. "Dropped in over all four remaining Zahurian landing sites." Zed frowned as something off screen caught his attention. Without even a "get going" Zed cut the connection.

"Shit!" Jay said, flicking on the light and sitting up. He wasn't going to need coffee now. His heart was racing faster than if he had run six blocks. The question was, what did the skimmer drop?

"We don't know what the skimmer dropped," Zed said five minutes later, after Elle had asked him.

Elle had managed, in less than five minutes, to jump into the shower and get dressed. Her tie was neatly tied, her shoes polished. Only her wet hair showed her haste.

Pro and his men looked more like Jay felt. They too had their suits on, but not a tie was in place and there were more wrinkles in their suits than in a rhino's hide. They looked more like men who had just come in from a strip bar than MiB agents ready to fight human–eating plum trees.

Jay had barely managed to get dressed after waking up Elle and Pro over the com line. At the moment he wished he'd taken the extra fifteen seconds to brush his teeth. Remembering his dream, he felt sure his breath smelled like rotten lettuce.

Around them, the war room seemed darker than usual, even though all the lights were on. The huge map covered with colored pins seemed almost out of place. The com screen linked to MiB headquarters was the size of a large television, and mounted in the panel of computers and other equipment. Everyone was standing around it so they all had a clear view.

"So, any possibilities?" Elle asked Zed. Behind their boss, the terminal looked to be doing normal business, as far as Jay could tell.

"Three," Zed said. "Weapons, Melenas, or both."

"How would the Zahurians retrieve weapons?" Jay asked.

"They wouldn't," Zed said. "At least not quickly or without help."

"And we'd find them first," Jay said.

Zed nodded. "More than likely. We've got agents covering the flight paths now."

"So it's probably Melenas," Elle said. "And most likely they'll be armed to rescue their masters."

"Right," Zed said.

"How come the ship didn't try to pick some of the meat-eaters up?" Elle asked.

Good question. Jay had been about to ask it.

Zed frowned. "We've had a lot of help in orbit, since we received word that Zahurians were spotted on Earth. At the moment we're keeping everyone who wants to help at bay. Containment nightmare."

Jay nodded. Aliens with a vendetta scouring the countryside were the last thing they needed.

"The skimmer didn't make it much farther than low orbit," Zed added, actually smiling, "before it became a cloud of dust. Wonderful sight."

"Gotcha," Jay said. "So how's about telling us what these plum-tree servants look like?"

"About to," Zed said. A moment later the screen filled with a picture of a bird-like creature. It had two clawed legs, two arms ending with clawed hands, and wings sprouting from its back. It had a long, sharp beak and wore a small vest with ammunition belts crossed over its chest. It carried what looked like a small rifle.

It was the meanest-looking bird Jay had ever seen.

Zed's voice came over the picture. "Melenas are the size of an Earth hummingbird, can hover and fly slowly backward. At full forward speed, they're faster than the human eye can follow. They communicate telepathically and are totally loyal to Zahurians."

"What kind of weapon is that?" Elle asked.

"Works like our AK-47," Zed said. "Bullets are the size of grains of sand, but they'll still poke holes in you if they hit you with enough of them. And they'll put out eyes, so glasses on for everyone at all times."

"Understood," Elle said.

"Hummingbird Rambos," Jay said, shaking his head. "Do they grunt?"

"No," Zed said, his face replacing the image of the Melena. "But their wings make a high-pitched screaming sound because of the thicker air here."

"So we'll hear them coming," Elle said.

"Not by much," Zed replied, "considering how fast they are."

"How many could that ship drop?"

"A thousand at each site," Zed said. "Maybe more."

"Any good news?" Jay asked.

"Yeah," Zed said. "They only live for three days, can't see at night, and are dumber than sheep.

Without a Zahurian guiding their attack telepathically, they won't be much of a threat."

"And with a tree as a guide?"

Zed only shrugged.

Jay hated it when Zed did that. It always meant, *figure it out yourself, kid, because you're in trouble.*

"How close do the trees have to be?" Elle asked, "so that they can guide the Melenas?"

Again Zed just shrugged. "No one knows. It's not in any of the files."

"Great," Jay said. "We're about to be attacked by a thousand hummingbirds with machine guns."

"Not before dawn," Zed said. "Good luck."

The screen clicked off, leaving the MiB agents listening to the silence of the night outside the warehouse. Suddenly very loud silence. Jay knew this had been too easy so far. But now the Zahurians had a weapon.

Elle looked at Jay, then at Pro, Partner, and Captain. "Any ideas?"

The containment crew shook their heads. Jay stared at Elle's face. Clearly she was a little shaken. "I have one," he said.

"What?" Elle asked.

"Breakfast," Jay said. "No point in dying on an empty stomach."

"Great idea," Pro said.

"But—" Elle started to protest, but Jay gently turned her and shoved her toward the kitchen that had been built into one side of the warehouse, just off the war room.

"Two hours before sunrise," he said. "We got time to eat."

Cistena could feel the excitement flowing through her traveling companions. Help had arrived. A ship had dropped Melenas, armed and ready to fight. Over a thousand now hovered above each site, waiting for the sun to come up. Now they had a chance.

Autropur figured it meant nothing. All the Melenas would do was buy them time to either run and hide, or to make a stand against the humans wearing black. And as the remainder of the night went on, the other Zahurians left from the first drop started to agree. Even with the swarm of Melenas hovering a thousand feet above the original drop site, it wasn't going to be enough. In a few Earth days the Melenas would be dead. They might be able to kill a few of the humans in black in the meantime, but that wouldn't stop the rest.

"We must join forces," one Zahurian argued. "Our weakness is in the fact that we are so spread out." And many of the group agreed.

Autropur did not. He was sure that their best defense was to stay separated and hidden.

He was argued down. The Zahurians agreed that they would join forces, using the cover of night to move, not eating so as not to leave tracks, and using the Melenas to distract the humans for a few days.

The two Zahurians who urged joining forces the most strenuously happened to be closest to the center of the remaining couples, so the joining would be near them. It would take time, but the Zahurians from the first drop would all come together in one place, collecting weapons as they went to fight the humans.

Autropur said they would not join the others, that they would remain hidden. Autropur didn't say that they would spend the next few nights moving even farther away from the landing site and their last kill.

Cistena was angry for the rest of the night at the decision, but the argument was kept shielded so that others could not hear. Autropur and Cistena had been mates for many years and they knew that at some things, Autropur was a better thinker. Cistena desperately wanted to be with the others, but would go along with Autropur's decision, at least for the moment.

Besides, Cistena's hopes were with the Melenas. Autropur told her to not think that way.

But Cistena did anyway. The Melenas had always been faithful servants and great fighters. They would stop the humans wearing black, teach them not to fight back against the great Zahurian race.

Autropur did not agree, so Cistena shut off the thoughts, raised her mental shields, and kept the ideas inside, like a dream. The dream was that after the Melenas had stopped the humans, they would continue their vacation, feasting at least twice a day until a ship came to pick them up and take them home. Maybe the dream was foolish, but it was still a dream.

There is no love sincerer than the love of food.

—GEORGE BERNARD SHAW

After breakfast, Jay and Elle spent the next hour before sunrise sitting in the war room planning two things: Which pair of Zahurians would they go after first, and how would they defend themselves against a swarm of Melenas that might have been dropped from the skimmer? There was no doubt that the Zahurians saw them coming, the Melenas would descend on them in a flash. And even though the Melenas had only tiny little weapons, Elle didn't much like the idea of getting hit with a hundred or so of those tiny bullets, let alone being swarmed by a thousand angry birds.

"So," she said, after they had decided which Zahurian pair to go after first, "how do we attack them?"

"Drive-by torching," Jay said.

16

"Huh?" Elle looked at her partner. Sometimes she was convinced he had lost his mind.

"Serious," he said. "The birds can't hurt us inside the MiB mobile. Right?" Everything on the LTD was bulletproof, including the tires. And that was from real, human-sized bullets. It was certainly not going to be hurt by bullets the size of sand, or by birds pecking at it.

Elle nodded and smiled as she caught on to his idea. Not a bad one, actually. "We keep Pro and the containment crew back and just kill the Zahurians from the car."

"Works for the Mafia," Jay said. "Should work for us, if we sneak up on the trees."

"And that might be the hardest thing to do," Elle said. She had a sneaking hunch she had just hit the problem on the head.

"That it might," Jay said. "But gettin' bird shit out of this suit would be even harder."

"Actually, I think blood would be worse," Elle said.

"Yeah," Jay said. "That, too."

Just before dawn, with Jay driving, they left the warehouse, traveling the dark roads of the Connecticut countryside. It seemed almost eerie to Elle, the sweep of their headlights on the empty roads. Lights were on in a few of the homes they passed, but this was too early for most folks in this area.

Two miles back, Pro and the containment crews followed. A safe distance, yet close enough to help if they were needed.

Elle hoped they wouldn't be needed for anything other than cleanup.

The sun was just sending streaks of red through the morning sky as they approached the first possible location of the two Zahurians. It was just outside a small village, along a fairly quiet back road. The only thing they had passed in the last mile was a pickup carrying a woman dressed in a business suit. Where she was going, Elle had no idea. But she sure gave them a hard look as she passed.

Both Jay and Elle kept staring up through the windshield at the sky. Elle wasn't sure exactly what they were looking for, but she would wager she would know it when she saw it.

Since they were the farthest east, she and Jay were the first agents to get sunlight. And since the Melenas could not function well at night, they were going to be the first agents to find out what was going to happen if Melenas had really been dropped by the skimmer. How they got that lucky task, she wasn't sure. She would have gladly passed it on to any of the other agents. She really wasn't that fond of birds in the first place. The were sort of like big rats with wings, as far as she was concerned.

She was also having a hard time imagining a thousand hummingbirds with machine-guns. She'd seen a lot of strange things since joining MiB Special Forces, and a lot before that in the morgue, but a thousand hummingbirds with machine-guns was going to be the strangest of them all. Assuming, of course, she lived through it.

"Anywhere along here," she said.

Jay slowed the LTD and both of them started scanning the surrounding trees and pastures. A few farms dotted the area, their white houses like ghosts in the morning light. A mist swirled off the fields, climbing toward the sky, promising another hot and humid spring day in the making.

The trail of this Zahurian twosome led from the small village they had just passed through and down this road. Each farm along the road had reported a missing animal, including the most recent disappearance from the farm they were now alongside.

If these two aliens stayed with their pattern, they would have moved down the road again last night, more than likely staying close to the tree line.

Jay and Elle missed them on the first pass.

Two miles up the road, Jay swung the LTD around and headed back. He figured that a few passes in this area would be enough, and then they'd moved on to the next report. With the possibility of the Melena swarm nearby, there wasn't any point in risking a search outside the car.

"There," Elle said, finally spotting them. She pointed at a clump of thick brush near the far side of a freshly plowed pasture.

At first Jay couldn't see what she was pointing at. Then he said, "Got it."

"Going in?" she asked, looking at the fence and shallow ditch between them and the field. She knew the LTD could handle just about anything, but that ditch looked deep. Almost too deep to get across, especially with mud everywhere.

"Goin' in," Jay said. "Hang on."

Jay gunned the LTD off the road and through the wire fence, pounding the car sideways into the ditch. The car banged hard, then jumped out of the ditch and into the plowed, brown-earth field. It took him a moment, but Jay got the LTD turned and headed straight at the aliens.

Elle figured that at best it was going to take them five seconds to get into position on the other side of the field, another few seconds to get out and burn down the brush and aliens, then a few more seconds to get back in the car.

The question was, did they have enough time before the Melena swarm arrived to protect their masters? Had they caught the trees by surprise?

Were there even Melenas around?

They were soon going to find out.

Jay slammed the car into a skid through the plowed field, sending dirt flying everywhere. Luckily, the field was still damp from the night air, or they would have been covered in a dust cloud and not able to see a thing.

While the car slid to a stop, Elle grabbed her Phaser from the backseat, making sure the setting was on wide. Flame-thrower.

Both she and Jay piled out of the LTD. Then she planted her feet in the dirt, leveled the Phaser at the brush and the aliens, and fired over the car door.

Jay fired at the same moment, and between the

two of them, the brush and aliens were ashes in seconds.

As Elle stopped firing, the sound of intense screaming reached her ears, filling the air like a thousand bad horror movies all playing at once.

The hummingbird cavalry was on the way.

"Shit!" Jay shouted.

Without even looking up, both she and Jay dove back into the car, slamming the doors behind them.

A second later the car was surrounded by thousands of birds, all firing at the car with tiny guns. If they'd been outside, Jay and Elle wouldn't have stood a chance.

Elle made sure all the doors were locked, just in case an alien hummingbird could open them. Then she and Jay just stared through the front windshield at the small, vicious creatures. There were so many of them that it seemed like night had descended around the LTD. And the noise was incredible. The high-pitched scream of their wings combined with the rumbling and pounding of their bodies and the machine-gun fire against the car.

Every so often one Melena paused just long enough for Elle to get a glimpse of the angry bird face, the tiny machine-gun, and the ammunition belts strapped across its chest.

"I feel like I'm in a Hitchcock movie," Elle shouted to Jay over the racket.

"Hitchcock on drugs," Jay shouted back.

The car rocked with the force of so many birds pounding against it. It wouldn't surprise Elle if there were enough of them to tip the car over. "Can you get us moving?" she shouted as the car began to rock wildly from side to side.

"Can't see to drive," Jay said. "But I got an idea."

Jay pointed at the switch for the car burglar system. It sent a current of high voltage electricity surging through the skin of the LTD, killing anything that touched it when the system was on. It was one of the first things Kay had told Jay about the car.

Elle nodded, yelling, "Do it!"

Jay flicked the switch.

Suddenly, the almost total darkness of the bird swarm was split by an electrical storm, like a bad night in the midwest. All they needed now was a tornado to pick them up and deposit them in Oz.

Sparks flew everywhere as smoke and explosions rocked the car. The Melenas were killed by the hundreds, their ammunition belts exploding along with their small bodies as the high voltage current cut them down if they even brushed a wing against the car.

After a moment the light streamed back into the car as the cloud of birds lifted, the survivors hovering in a mass a hundred feet above the car, regrouping.

"Wow," Jay said, digging a finger in his ear to ease some of the ringing.

"That was loud," Elle said, staring at the incredible sight around them.

The LTD was surrounded by smoke from burning bird bodies. The hood of the car was a good half a foot deep in bodies, all frying like roasters on a barbecue. Only these roasters had small guns and ammunition belts that would explode every so often with a pop, scattering more feathers.

"I'm going to report what just happened to Zed and the others," Elle said. "They need to know that the skimmer dropped Melenas, and how little time they have."

"Tell 'em not to get out of the car." Jay looked up at the birds overhead.

Elle looked too, and was suddenly struck by another idea. She glanced at Jay, who was shaking his head while craning his neck. Her idea was crazy, but it just might work. Through the blood and feather-splattered windshield, she could see the cloud of Melenas hovering over them. It was a huge cloud. All the frying birds on the car hadn't seemed to cut down their mass or power. And something needed to.

"Got a thought," Elle said.

"What?" Jay asked.

"I'm going to grab us a couple Noisy Crickets."

Jay looked at her with a frown.

She stuck her hand out and cocked her wrist, like she had done on the firing range with the Cricket, her index finger extended. Then she slowly turned her pointed finger upward.

He stared at her for a moment, then broke out into laughter, pounding the dash in approval.

Elle quickly climbed over the backseat and flipped down the panel that gave access to the trunk. A moment later she handed him one of the tiny guns that had caused him so much grief.

"This ain't gonna break my wrist?" he asked, holding the gun gingerly between two fingers.

Elle laughed. "Positive. When held right, it has no kick."

"Okay," Jay said, taking the gun in his left hand.

"I'm turning off the burglar repellent system," Elle said, flicking the switch on the dashboard. "Then we go on three. One for roll down the window. Two for hands out. Fire on three."

Jay nodded.

"One."

Both of them lowered their windows just enough to get an arm out.

"Two."

As if one body, both of them leaned forward to stare out the front windshield at the cloud of birds above as they stuck their hands out the side windows and pointed the guns upward.

"Three," Elle said.

Both fired.

"Feel anything?" Elle asked, not looking at him.

"Not even the slightest kick," he said. "Amazing."

Overhead the result was clear. Two large overlapping holes had appeared in the cloud of birds as both of their shots cleaned out hundreds of the creatures in a massive explosion of feathers and alien blood.

"Again," Jay said, and pulled the trigger.

More of the birds disappeared.

Elle fired.

Jay fired.

The remaining birds kept forming a smaller and smaller swarm, not able to understand what was happening. Zed was right, they were dumber than sheep.

With two final shots, the swarm was gone.

Elle stared up through the windshield, waiting, as the massive rain of blood and feathers covered the field around them. From what she could see, no more birds had appeared. There might be a few stragglers, but they could certainly handle just a few. Their numbers had made them deadly.

Slowly, she and Jay climbed out of the LTD. A thousand blown-up Melena bodies was something to see. In front of the car the brush where the two Zahurians had been continued to burn. Feathers drifted from the sky like snow.

"This is going to be a fun cleanup," Elle said.

"Yeah. Time to call Zed. You want to do it?"

"Go ahead," Elle said. "Make sure you tell him about the Cricket."

Jay pointed a finger at her and nodded, then climbed back into the LTD.

Elle looked from the mass of dead birds to the small gun in her hand. A thousand hummingbirds with machine-guns blown out of the air by two Noisy Crickets. Could this job get any stranger?

That which is never attempted never transpires.

—JACK VANCE

Jay and Elle found no more Zahurians that day, and didn't see another hummingbird with a machine-gun. Sort of a good news, bad news end to the day.

The agents at the other three Zahurian drop sites were able to use Jay and Elle's experience with the Melenas to their advantage. All stayed inside their cars and all destroyed the swarms of gun-toting birds with Noisy Crickets. No agent was hurt.

Good news.

By the end of the day, there were only four Zahurians left at the North Dakota drop site, six at the Minnesota site, a full dozen in Michigan, and twenty in Connecticut. Forty-two out of 208. The humans were winning. Jay figured it would only be a matter of time before all the meat-eaters were

17

gone. But how many more people would die? Jay tried to concentrate on the positive. The minute they got back to the war room, Jay knew they were in trouble.

"Shit," he said, standing near the fax machine. "Figured it out."

"Figured what out?" Elle said, dropping into a chair and putting her feet up.

"How we're trackin' em," Jay said. He pointed to the fax machine.

"Empty?" Elle asked.

"Echoes. Nothing more." No pet, farm animal, or human had gone missing in their area in almost a day. No human had been killed and eaten. That was good news. But having no way to track the meat-eaters was very bad news.

Jay sat down beside Elle and stared at the map. For the pair they'd killed this morning, Elle had replaced the colored pins with black ones. But there were still a lot of colored pins up there, and the Zahurians had gone into hiding. They were going to be damn near impossible to find very soon.

"Night hunting?" Elle said. "Catch them moving?"

"Seems like we got no choice," Jay said.

"Dinner, plan our hits, then head out?" Elle asked.

He nodded tiredly. "Yeah. You tell Pro."

"Sure thing," Elle said, pushing herself up from her chair and heading for the back room.

Jay stared at the colored pins for a moment longer, then followed her. At least he was going to get a good dinner. No sleep, but food. Another good news, bad news sort of thing. It had been that kind of day.

The LTD had hundreds of great features, only one of which was its night-sight abilities. The headlights and spotlights could be flipped to ultraviolet and the windshield and windows converted to the equivalent of night goggles. Since the car was black and had a silent running feature, on a dark night it was almost invisible. Tonight the LTD would be nothing more than a fleeting shadow.

Elle and Jay switched over to dark running about a half mile from a possible Zahurian location on a back road. If they saw another car coming, they would simply pull off to the side of the road and stop. But this road looked like it wasn't used much.

Inside the LTD, Elle and Jay looked out as if it were almost daylight. Jay used one ultraviolet spotlight while Elle used another, scanning the tree-line and fields with even brighter light. Zed figured they didn't have much of a chance, since more than likely the Zahurians could see ultraviolet, but he had given them permission to try. "What the hell," was what he said exactly.

They spent almost an hour at one site, finding nothing, before moving to the next possible location near a mortuary. They searched that area for over an hour, then moved on without finding anything.

By four in the morning, they had searched five

possible Zahurian locations and were both too tired to care about their lack of success. The last thing Jay remembered before falling into his bed as the sun painted the sky orange outside the warehouse was Zed saying. "Meeting at six tonight in my office. Get some sleep."

Jay dreamed of birds. Talking birds, pointing Noisy Crickets at him with their claws, always keeping one claw extended in just the right manner.

The complete destruction of the Melenas sent Cistena into a long silence, her thoughts sealed off. She was also upset about the slow torture of two of her friends by the humans in black. The humans had been trying to send a message. And as far as Cistena was concerned, it was loud and clear. She wasn't going near any human ever again if she could help it.

Autropur had learned that when Cistena sealed her thoughts, it was best just to leave well enough alone. Finally, as the day drew to a close and the welcome relief of night covered them, Cistena opened up again.

"It would not have mattered," Autropur thought directly at his mate. "The Melenas could not have done anything for us, except get us a little more time."

"I know," Cistena thought back. "I had just hoped that the Melenas would hurt the humans, pay them back for killing our companions."

"We have killed many of them," Autropur said.

"That is different," Cistena shot back. "They are food. They are made to be eaten."

Autropur remained silent, his thoughts kept inside, until finally Cistena asked, "What do we do now?"

"We remain here," Autropur thought, putting some power behind his message. "We cannot be found here, so we will not move."

At that moment a warning thought came in from another Zahurian couple. "The humans are hunting at night!"

Cistena aimed a tight response at Autropur. "How?"

Autropur did not know. And Cistena knew Autropur did not know. So, for the rest of the night, the two Zahurians remained hidden, deep inside the brush and trees of an Earth forest. At one point, intense artificial light swept over the edge of their hiding place, but nothing was disturbed. Autropur and Cistena did not move to see what caused the light.

The night ended with no more of their companions being killed by the humans. Cistena seemed almost buoyant as the sun covered her purple flowers. Even Autropur relaxed a little, and for the first time in two Earth days, he thought it might be possible to live through this attack.

On the bridge of a large Grayhawkian spaceship hovering just outside the orbit of Pluto, Raptor-Six approached Raptor-Five in the standard manner of an inferior approaching a superior. Both heads were bowed, all four arms were sucked up against the chest, all four eye-stalks were tucked tight against the skin, both eyelids on all eyes down.

The thin, hot atmosphere of the ship gave everything a yellow brightness, fading into green. Around Raptor-Five, a thick, shape-forming chair supported him as he faced a screen that showed a map of the system in front of them. Four Haaacks, their two tentacles constantly moving, stood ready in front of large bags full of sticks. Those Haaacks, with those sticks, ran the ship, and Raptor-Five ran the Haaacks. It had been a smooth running ship for six Earth years now and Raptor-Five had no intentions of changing that.

"R-Five," R-Six said, moving his hands above his head in a wide sweeping gesture, a standard salute. "The enemies of the Zahurian Race continue to gather."

"How many?" R-Five asked.

"Nine races with warships such as ours," R-Six said. "All are waiting, as we are."

R-Five tipped one eye-stalk sideways in a motion that said he understood. Since it had become known that a group of Zahurians were trapped on the primitive planet Earth, every enemy of the Zahurians had sent ships. R-Five desperately wanted to kill a plant creature, watch it curl up and die, its leaves flaking to dust in the hot sun. He had no doubt the other races gathered here would enjoy the same.

But his reason was personal. The Zahurians had

eaten his ninth wife, Talon-Nine, leaving him wanting, angry. Even nine more wives later, he still wanted revenge on the plants.

"Report from R-Seven?"

"Nothing yet," R-Six said. "He will be arriving at the Earth station in a short time. He will not be the first. Other races are going in, requesting the same."

R-Five again tipped an eye-stalk. First he would ask permission to help hunt the Zahurians. It was the correct thing to do under the treaty that governed this planet. But if the humans were stupid enough to refuse a member of the Grayhawkian race, then they would hunt the Zahurians anyway.

Talon-Nine would be avenged. The score would be settled, the debt paid. No stupid humans would get in his way.

Between two evils, I always pick the one I never tried before.

—MAE WEST

The Immigration Center was busier than Jay had ever seen it. And louder. The usual dull roar was now approximating Grand Central Station during five o'clock rush hour.

Mixing with the dozens of familiar alien races were a dozen races Jay had never seen before, including a two-headed, four-armed ugly mother, with red skin that looked like it was constantly peeling. Jay hoped he'd never have a run-in with that one in a dark alley. Or a lit alley, for that matter.

The Twins looked harried, their tentacles moving over the big board faster than Jay could remember them ever moving. The pictures on the big screen flashed past quicker than Jay could follow. And the Twin's clicking language sounded more like a telegraph than anything understandable.

18

Even Zed was starting to look tired. That surprised Jay the most. Zed hadn't looked tired since Jay's first mission with Kay against the bug.

"Chairs," Zed said as Jay, Elle, and seven other MiB agents filed into his office. Zed punched a button on his desk. The windows turned black, then the door closed.

Zed pushed another button and nodded to himself.

Jay grabbed a chair near the wall and leaned back, waiting. Calling all the agents in from the field was rare. Normally, information could be passed by phone. This was clearly something unusual.

"No one's going to overhear this meeting," Zed said, checking his panel one more time, then glancing up at the agents.

"Dirty movies?" Jay asked, and nodded his head at the darkened windows.

No one laughed, and Zed ignored him. Tough crowd.

Jay looked around the room. The other agents here, including Dee and Ess, were in charge of the other Zahurian sites. They all looked as worn out as Jay felt. The four hours of sleep this morning just hadn't done it for him. He wagered some of them, since they were farther west, had gotten even less sleep. And less sleep with thirty-seven hour days was a real killer.

"Update," Zed said, standing beside his desk. "Only two of the meat-eating bastards left in North Dakota. I'm pulling out all agents except Dee and

Ess and moving them to Michigan, since there are only four left in Minnesota."

Everyone nodded, including Jay. The plan made sense. Focus a large number of agents in one area, clean up the problem, then focus on the next area. So far, it was working. But now they had to figure out another way of tracking the Zahurians.

"So," Zed said, moving around behind his desk and sitting down. "To the reason I called you all in here."

"I'm still hopin' for a movie," Jay said.

Again Zed ignored him, and Elle slapped his arm, warning him to be serious.

Zed flicked a switch on his desk and a panel in the wall near Jay opened. Jay almost jumped out of his chair. He didn't even know there was a secret door there, let alone where it led. This place was constantly surprising him.

A short, red-skinned alien stepped from the secret panel and stood beside Zed. The alien had a pig face, black eyes, and smelled really, really bad, almost like a New York sewer, only worse. He wore a bright pink robe with nothing on his hoofed feet. Two black horns extended from his forehead, making him look very much like pictures of the devil. All he needed was a pitchfork and the cliché would be complete.

In all the MiB training films and manuals, Jay had never seen this race pictured. Another fun MiB surprise.

Secret panels, new races, what was next?

Jay wasn't the only agent surprised by the alien.

Almost all of them seemed to be. Elle looked pale, as if she had just seen a ghost. And the smell of the alien seemed to gag her. The fact that he wasn't the only one bothered by the stench made Jay feel a little better, but not much.

"I want you to meet Bob," Zed said.

Jay snorted, then said, "Bob?" aloud before he realized he'd even spoken. What a funny name for an alien who looked like a cross between Porky Pig and the Devil.

The alien looked directly at him, its cold, black eyes seeming to cut through Jay like a paring knife. All Jay could think was that the alien was very creepy, and most certainly dangerous.

At that you are right.

The thought was as clear as if the creep with the pig face and horns was speaking, but it was only inside Jay's head.

"Shit!" Jay said. In all his years he'd never had someone climb inside his head and he didn't much like it. "Stop that!"

Zed grunted. "I see Jay has discovered our guest's secret. Bob here is a telepath, from a race of telepaths called Neleks."

"Stay da hell out of my mind," Jay said, glaring at the pig-faced alien.

Gladly.

The thought was like a slap. The invasion made Jay want to run to the nearest hot shower and let the water run over him. He actually shivered.

"Bob," Zed said. "We agreed you would use language with the agents."

Bob nodded, then with one last glare at Jay, he said through his translator, "I am pleased to be working with you."

"Bob here," Zed said, almost touching the alien on the shoulder and then thinking better of it, "is going to help us track Zahurians."

"I can sense them from great distances," Bob said. Even though Jay was five steps from Bob, he would swear he could smell his breath. Sulfur and rot. This guy was going to be real fun to work with.

"Neleks," Zed said, "are mortal enemies of the Zahurians."

And vice-versa, Jay bet, but didn't say anything.

Bob nodded, again looking at Jay. Jay managed not to shiver this time, and stayed silent.

"He'll be going to the North Dakota site first," Zed said. "Then working his way east as the Zahurians are cleaned up. People, I've got to tell you, we don't have much time here."

Jay glanced at Elle, who only shrugged.

"You want to explain that, boss?" Ess asked.

Zed pointed at the dark window in the direction of the Immigration Center. "So far we've got two dozen races who want revenge against the Zahurians. Many more are on the way."

"What do they want from us?" Ess asked.

"They are all asking for permission to hunt Zahurians," Zed said. "We're not going to be able to stall them much longer. If you don't find and kill every Zahurian left here within a few days, a week at most, this part of Earth will become open season, with races fighting each other for the privilege of hunting here."

"And Bob's race has won the lottery?" Jay asked.

"His presence stays a secret," Zed said, frowning at Jay. "Word gets out that a Nelek is helping us and we'll have a hundred ships not bothering to ask permission."

Bob gave what Jay suspected was a smile, but it turned out to be more like an ugly grimace. "My people are hated as much as the Zahurians by the races in this sector of the galaxy."

"Great," Jay said so only Elle could hear. "We've made a deal with the devil."

Exactly.

The thought echoed in Jay's mind and he knew, without a doubt, that the next time he closed his eyes he wouldn't be having nightmares about moving vegetables and birds. In fact, he doubted he was ever going to sleep again. Safer that way.

Autropur thought Cistena was going to panic, run into the human road, and give their location away. Somehow, with calming thoughts, Autropur managed to keep Cistena standing quietly in the middle of the forest. Yet Autropur had never felt such fear, horror, and just plain dread. And the feeling was flowing through all their remaining traveling companions. For them, it was a cultural fear, running deeper than simple thought.

It was instinct.

A Nelek had arrived on Earth.

Nothing worse could have happened.

"Calm." Autropur's powerful thought spread through the other Zahurians left near the first landing site. "Calm!"

Slowly, all twenty Zahurians blocked the fear from the others and calmed down, listening to Autropur's repeated thought. Finally, when all were listening, Autropur presented a plan.

"Human thoughts are so primitive that a lot of them would drown out our presence, hiding us from a Nelek," Autropur thought clearly at them all. "We must all hide together, where there are a lot of humans, where each Zahurian can help his companion keep as mentally quiet as possible. It will be our only hope."

His plan sent many questions through the others. How could they hide with humans when it was the humans who were killing them?

"Only humans wearing black," Autropur answered. "Many human trees look exactly like us. Only we must not eat, or move when approached. Then even the humans in black cannot tell."

Around Autropur and Cistena the sun set, covering them with darkness and a slight feeling of security. But in the background, they could all sense the Nelek, their mortal enemy. The Nelek was still some distance away, but they had to get to safety quickly. And on this world, the only place safe from a telepath was among the primitive thoughts of humans. Autropur couldn't sense human thoughts, and had no desire to. But a Nelek was an animal. He did not have the luxury of not hearing the humans' thoughts. And that would be the Zahurians' salvation.

With Autropur's prompting, each Zahurian pair thought about the human gathering places they had seen. Finally, they chose a huge structure full of Earth trees that looked like they did. It would be an easy task to replace those trees with Zahurians and hide among thousands of humans. Very easy.

The difficult task was going to be getting there. For many of the Zahurians, the distance to the huge structure was great, and the risks high during the journey, especially with the humans in black hunting at night. But the risk of being found by a Nelek was much worse than death at the hands of the humans. Neleks turned a Zahurian mind inside out. Being killed by a Nelek was the most painful thing any of them could imagine.

"We start now," Autropur said. "Do we all agree?"

Cistena hesitated for a moment, then added agreement into the flowing thoughts.

Autropur sent Cistena a comforting thought, then started through the thick brush and trees that had hidden them for days. Their travel would take a number of Earth days. But, with luck, they would make it to a place where they could live for a long, long time among the humans. In a huge building they called Mall.

> *The absurd is the essential concept and the first truth.*
>
> — ALBERT CAMUS

The next three days were the longest and most frustrating days Jay could ever remember living. He and Elle spent from dawn to late each night searching the Connecticut countryside for Zahurians and coming up completely blank. No animal or human had gone missing, and neither of them could figure out how to track the meat-eating trees without the police reports. It was as if the twenty aliens had simply vanished, or left the planet.

Jay knew they couldn't be so lucky.

Bob, the Nelek, had found the two remaining Zahurians in North Dakota in one day, and had seemed almost angry, from what Jay had heard, when the two agents burned the Zahurians down. It was as if Bob

19

wanted something more. Jay didn't even want to imagine what that might be.

In Minnesota, the remaining four Zahurians were tracked down, again with Bob's help, in two days. They were also all burned.

Now, on the fourth morning after the meeting in Zed's office, Bob had moved to Michigan, where there were ten Zahurians left when he arrived. Jay and Elle had hoped to clear out the Zahurians in Connecticut, so as not to have to work with the Nelek. But it was becoming more and more obvious that that wasn't going to happen. They were just going to have to deal with the creepy alien bastard.

Elle sipped her coffee, staring at the now worthless and out-of-date information on their huge map. Jay sat beside her. To him it seemed pointless to search blindly through forty thousand square miles where twenty small trees might be hiding. Even with Pro's containment team running search patterns at the same time, their chances of stumbling across any of the aliens were slim to none.

"Where'd they go?" Elle muttered, more to herself than Jay. It was about the hundredth time one or the other of them had asked the question, as if repeating it might somehow provide an answer.

"At least no more people are dying," Jay said.

"At the moment," Elle said.

"Yeah," Jay said. "At the moment."

The communication link beeped. Jay climbed slowly to his feet and moved to answer it, punching up full visual. Zed's tired face appeared on the screen.

"Bob found two more trees," Zed said.

"Good for horned boy," Jay said.

Zed frowned, then went on. "You got trouble heading your way real fast."

"Bob's comin' early, huh?"

Elle jumped to her feet and joined Jay. "What kind of trouble?"

"Grayhawkian warship coming in without permission. None of the other warships are stopping it."

"And it's coming here?" Elle asked.

Zed nodded. "To hunt Zahurians."

"Great," Jay said. "More telepaths."

"No." Zed shook his head. "Just bozos who hate Zahurians enough to risk a ship and crew to hunt them. We're holding the other races off so far." Zed laughed. "Actually, they're holding each other off, just waiting to see what we do. If we let the Grayhawkians in, it might open the floodgates before Bob can clean up the trees and get off the planet."

"Containment hell," Jay said.

"Exactly," Zed agreed.

"So what are we going to do?" Elle asked.

Zed sighed. "Warn them off if you can."

"Is that gonna work?" Jay asked.

"Not likely," Zed said.

"Then what?"

"Blow the suckers off the planet," Zed said, his expression neutral.

Elle smiled. "Just wanted to be clear."

"I'll send in extra containment crews to help Pro," Zed said. "Good luck."

The screen went dead. A moment later data poured in over the computer net, showing the exact location the Grayhawkian ship intended to land, and when. Also how to stop the warship, what to expect from the aliens themselves, and why. Much more data than they were going to have time for. And a picture of what a Grayhawkian looked like.

"I'll be," Jay said, holding up the picture of the four-armed alien with red, peeling skin. "The ugly mother from the Immigration Center."

"Noticed him, too, huh?" Elle said, laughing.

"Hard ta miss."

"Two miles from here." Elle shook her head as she read the data coming in over the computer. "Right near the place where the Zahurians were dropped."

"How long?"

"Twenty minutes."

"Print that stuff and let's boogie," Jay said, heading for the garage area of the old warehouse at a run. "You can read it to me on the way."

For the first time in days they actually had something real to do. Jay had to admit, it felt damned good.

Raptor-Five watched as the Haaacks adjusted a few sticks and moved the great warship down into the Earth's atmosphere. It would only be a short time before they were on the ground, and the sacred

Zahurian hunt would begin. It would be glorious, to finally get his revenge for what happened to Talon-Nine.

Raptor-Six stood a prescribed distance away from Raptor-Five, also watching. But his four arms were moving in gentle circles, his four eye-stalks waving back and forth with worry. He did not agree with his commander's decision to take the mighty warship to the surface of the planet. There it would have little protection, like a great bird having to fight only on its feet.

He had objected, as was his duty. R-Five had brushed his objections aside with a roll of his four eye-stalks and a circle of his four arms.

"We are being warned away by the humans," the second communications Haaack reported.

"Ignore the warning," R-Five said, his arms flailing in his anger at having to speak to a lowly Haaack. "Continue with the landing."

R-Six let his eye-stalks roll even more, showing his increasingly strong objections.

R-Five just ignored his second in command, focusing instead on the screen showing the blue, green, and white of the planet below. There were no reds in evidence. No rock. No beautiful desert. Just blue oceans and green plants. An ugly planet, to be sure. But if Zahurians were here, he didn't care. Revenge was all the beauty he needed.

"Six strokes until touchdown," the chief navigating Haaack said, twisting one control stick while pulling out another.

Raptor-Five bent both heads forward in understanding. "Continue."

Raptor-Six almost moaned aloud, but caught himself in time. Such a show of disrespect would have gotten his eye-stalks pulled out. His commander had made a decision, it was his job to support him, even if he was wrong. But he still kept his arms moving slowly in circles to show his concern.

Below, the green and blue planet raced toward the huge warship. Raptor-Five watched the screen, drool slipping from his two mouths as he anticipated the coming hunt. There was nothing better than killing Zahurians.

Nothing. Not even a sand stick struck in the great Grayhawkian desert. Not even that.

Nothing was better.

"Big mother," Jay said as he stared up into the blue morning sky at the huge Grayhawkian ship dropping quickly toward the ground. Luckily for Pro and the rest of the containment crews, the ship had picked a pretty open area to land. So far less than a dozen farmers and passers-by had stopped to stare. Pro and his crews were spread out among them, holding Phaser rifles, keeping the onlookers under control and making sure none of them left before they were flashed.

"You ain't kidding," Elle said. "Size of a football field, at the very least."

Actually, Jay was surprised that the ship was shaped almost exactly *like* a football field. It was rectangular, thicker in the middle than at the end, and seemed to have no front or back. There were also no windows or obvious doors. Just a huge, flat sheet of shining metal.

Then, with a loud snap that echoed over the countryside like a clap of thunder, four openings in the huge ship appeared. Four legs extended from its underside and a moment later the ship settled to the ground, covering two pastures and smashing a small group of pine trees.

"Smooth touchdown," Jay said.

"You were expecting something else?" Elle asked.

The ship must have been powered by an anti-gravity system, since there weren't any rockets visible, and nothing seemed to shut off when it stopped. It just sort of sat there, when a moment before it had been floating in the air. Impressive.

"Wonder where the front is?" Elle said.

"Damn good question." Jay shifted his Phaser rifle to the notch of his left arm. It was fully charged and ready to go. Elle also had a Phaser rifle on her arm.

"One weak spot is above the legs," Elle said, pointing. "That's what research said, anyhow."

"Or a door," Jay added. Firing a Phaser rifle at the metal hull of an interstellar warship wasn't going to do much. More than likely it wouldn't even leave a mark. But a full Phaser shot into a hatch or another opening might do some real damage.

"Yeah, that too," Elle agreed. "Even better."

"So," Jay said, stepping toward the ship. "Let's

go knock on a leg and see if we can get 'em to open up."

It turned out they didn't need to knock. Jay had taken about ten steps into the plowed field when a popping sound echoed over the trees and a seam in the metal appeared on the underside of the ship. Within a few seconds, a shallow-sloped ramp had formed, leading from the interior of the craft to the dirt of the farmer's field.

Jay and Elle moved up to the edge of the ramp and waited, staring up into the darkness inside.

Above them the ship loomed like a massive metal ceiling ready to fall and crush them at any moment. A smell, like burning popcorn, overpowered the spring morning fragrance of the countryside.

"Wow," Elle said. "Nice odor."

Nothing inside the ship was moving, so Jay and Elle simply stood there, rifles resting across their arms, trying not to choke on the smell. Jay had no doubt he wasn't going to be eating popcorn for some time to come.

After about five minutes, Elle turned to Jay. "Maybe they want us to go in."

"And have that smell ruin every movie for me for the rest of my life?" Jay said. "No chance, sister. I'm stayin' here."

It took another ten minutes before something finally emerged from the ship. An alien, looking exactly like the one they had seen in the Immigration Center, started down the ramp. He had two heads, four arms, eyes on stalks, and peeling, red skin. He wore a red robe with white bands. There didn't seem to be an expression on either face, but the eye-stalks were moving in a certain controlled fashion, and all four arms were also jerking, as if the motion meant something. More than likely it did.

Jay's language translator made no sound, so Jay figured the guy wasn't actually talking yet.

Behind him was another Grayhawkian, almost as large. And behind him were dozens of smaller, lizard-like creatures carrying bags full of weird-looking sticks.

"Those creatures are called Haaacks," Elle said, indicating the lizards. "I think they're servants, or some sort of lower race." Elle had read what she could of the data sheets while Jay drove from the warehouse.

"Caddies," Jay said.

Elle laughed. "Looks like it."

"You are not welcome here on Earth," Jay said as the Grayhawkian approached. Jay talked slowly enough for his translator to convert his speech into the clicks, whistles, and beeps of the Grayhawkian language. "Please leave now."

The creature in front stopped about twenty paces up the shallow ramp from Jay, its arms spinning in circles above its head. After a moment, the language translator said simply, "Eat excrement, humans. I come for Zahurians."

Jay looked at Elle, then let his mouth drop open in a sign of mock shock.

Elle was just barely covering her smile. "That ugly alien there just told us to eat shit."

"What are we gonna do about it?" Jay asked, grinning at his partner.

"Toast them?" Elle asked.

"I love toast in the mornin'," Jay said.

He turned back to the two-headed alien standing on the ramp.

"I'd say," Jay said, spacing his words as he lifted his Phaser rifle without aiming it at the Grayhawkian, "that from the looks of you, you've eaten enough shit for both of us."

Just as the translator finished, both Jay and Elle aimed their Phaser rifles and fired.

The leader exploded like a balloon touched by a pin.

The smell suddenly changed from burning popcorn to rotted chicken.

The Grayhawkian behind the leader exploded in the same way an instant later, splattering the two agents with brownish, foul blood. One of the Grayhawkian heads rolled clear of the ship and bounced in the dirt.

The two, tight-beamed Phaser shots disintegrated the lizards—sticks, bags and all, like they had never existed.

"Hit it hard!" Jay shouted, aiming the Phaser rifle at the insides of the ship.

He kept his finger on the Phaser's trigger, sending more destructive energy into the ship than he cared to imagine. He'd never seen anything that could withstand a constant Phaser blast.

Elle aimed her rifle at the same place and matched his shot, doubling the energy.

For a moment, the two agents stood firing, covered in Grayhawkian blood, surrounded by the smell of rotting meat and burnt popcorn.

Then, slowly, the ship started to rumble.

"Run for it!" Jay shouted.

Elle slipped in the slime and blood, but Jay had her by the arm and back on her feet before she even hit the dirt. At full speed the two of them headed for the car.

Along the side road, Pro and the rest of the containment crews ordered all the onlookers to take cover. Humans and MiB agents alike hit the ditches and hid behind cars.

Jay and Elle cleared the edge of the ship just as the first explosion shook it.

They reached the car as the second explosion rocked the ground around them.

They stopped to watch.

For a moment, it looked as if the ship might be trying to lift off, even with the internal explosions. The ramp started to retract, laboriously disappearing into the ship.

"Damn!" Elle said. "We didn't hit it enough."

"In the pits," Jay said, bringing his Phaser rifle back up into firing position. He aimed at the closest point where the legs extended from the skin of the ship. He hit it dead center, first try, and continued to pour energy in, again holding the trigger in the full power position.

Elle, a moment later, aimed at the opening on the right side of the ship, nailing it first shot.

Another large explosion rocked the ship and the ramp stopped retracting.

Suddenly the area that Jay had been firing at seemed to turn to melted cheese. The leg slipped upward into the ship like a sword through a plate of mush. The entire ship tipped to the left.

Another explosion shot flame down the partially extended ramp.

The leg Elle had been firing at seemed to lose its support as well. The ship rocked and tipped back the other way as the right leg seemed to crumple up inside the hull.

Finally, a huge explosion split the air and both Jay and Elle quit firing, standing beside the LTD as the huge Grayhawkian warship shuddered and died, one explosion at a time.

Jay flipped open his pocket phone and said, "Give me Zed."

The two legs of the ship closest to them buckled completely and the entire thing nose-dived into the field, shaking the car and sending a huge, echoing boom rolling over the countryside.

"Wow!" Elle said.

"That seems to have worked," Jay said, smiling. The huge ship now looked more like a giant metal hill than a spaceship. Maybe Pro would leave it for the kids to ski on in the winter. Hell, it looked slick enough to ski on now.

"Go ahead," Zed said.

"One toasted Grayhawkian battle cruiser."

"Perfect," Zed said. "That will buy us some

time. Good work." The phone went dead as Zed cut the connection.

"What'd he say?" Elle asked.

"That we should take the afternoon off."

"He didn't."

"Yeah," Jay said. "He didn't. But we done deserve it."

Elle looked back at the huge Grayhawkian battle cruiser as another explosion ripped through its interior. "We do, don't we?"

"Now the woman be talkin'."

As it turned out, they ended up helping Pro with containment for the next six hours before the hulk of the Grayhawkian battle cruiser was lifted back into space and sent into the sun. Jay couldn't remember a time when his flashy-thing got such a workout. After a while, he didn't even bother to take off the sunglasses in between flashes.

Pro finally sent Jay and Elle back to the warehouse when he caught Jay telling a recently flashed man that he hadn't seen an alien spaceship, he'd seen the Rockettes practicing a nude routine in the field.

"Remember the great high kicks," Jay had said as Pro led the man away for reflashing.

On Jay's first day in MiB, Kay had told Jay about fighting the scum of the universe. Kay forgot to mention how much of a pain in the butt the cleanup after the fight was. Especially with someone like Pro taking all the fun out of it.

The world is a stage, but the play is badly cast.

— OSCAR WILDE

Cistena and Autropur had hidden for most of the day in a deep grouping of trees and then, as night set, had started out again.

Now they were on the edge of a vast, well-lit open area around the huge human building. Soon they would cross the openness and move inside. But for the moment, they had to wait. There were still too many humans moving about.

For three days they had been on the move, hiding most of the day, making great time toward the arranged meeting place at night. They were one short evening's travel away from their destination, if nothing interfered.

During the day Cistena had alternated between excitement at their progress and depression when the Nelek found another of

20

their companions at the other drop sites. There were very few of them left. What had been a mind full of thoughts not many Earth days before now seemed empty, with almost no thoughts to fill Cistena's days and nights. Autropur also had problems with the emptiness. It was going to be all they could do just to survive the next few days. Cistena had to stay calm and thinking clearly, somehow.

So far, six of their companions had made it into the huge human structure that stood across the open area from where they now hid. They had relayed that it was a perfect hiding place. There were hundreds of the human trees that looked just like them scattered throughout the building, planted in large pots, with lots of cover for Zahurian roots. Every day, from early in the morning until late in the evening, the mall was filled with humans, whose primitive thoughts would block the Nelek's telepathic abilities. But during the hours the humans stayed away, they would have to remain fully mentally blocked, helping each other to keep from letting even a stray thought out.

The only problem for the first Zahurians had been getting into the mall and moving into position without being detected. Finally, by standing near a door that humans used and waiting patiently, they had been able to move inside and into position early in the morning, a little at a time. They had all decided to go inside using the same method as the first. It was better than having one Zahurian inside risk detection by moving to open a door.

Autropur hoped there wouldn't be any problems

for him and Cistena, either. They would soon find out. They would be against the outer wall of the mall before the night was over.

For the first time since the Nelek arrived on the planet, Autropur felt there was a possibility that they might survive, and Cistena echoed those sentiments. But still, just the idea of a Nelek here on Earth made Autropur shiver and lose leaves. Autropur had no idea why the humans would allow a Nelek to land, let alone work with one. Clearly, humans were totally stupid.

Of course, the humans had wiped out most of the Zahurians without the Nelek's help, so clearly they were not as primitive as they seemed.

Cistena and Autropur froze in position along the tree-line as a human vehicle sped past, then they moved on. Soon they would be standing among hundreds of humans, safer than they had been in many days. All they had to do was move across the vast open space, get inside the locked building, and then replace an Earth tree. All without being seen.

They would make it. They had no other choice.

"Destroying the Grayhawkian ship bought us almost nothing," Zed said, his face filling the communication screen.

"Oh, great," Jay said. "Risk our lives, and for what?"

"A good night's sleep," Elle said, yawning.

"Oh, yeah," Jay said. "That." He grinned at Elle as she sipped her coffee. They had managed, after helping Pro and the containment crews clean up the mess, to get to bed early and get a decent night's sleep. For Jay, it had lasted, almost without dreams, right up until Zed's wake-up call. He and Elle now sat, fully dressed in their black suits and ties, in front of the communication panel. Jay was almost ready for a full thirty-seven more hours.

"There are only four Zahurians left at the Michigan site," Zed said. "Bob should have them spotted by late afternoon."

"Good for devil-boy," Jay said.

"I wouldn't be saying, or even thinking, things like that tonight," Zed said, smiling.

"Shit." Elle stared down into her coffee.

"See," Jay said. "Just the thought of Bob showin' up curdles cream."

"Well, smart-ass," Zed said, "you work with him. We got to find those Zahurians."

"More landings?" Elle asked.

"A half-dozen last night," Zed said. "Who knows how many might try tonight. I pulled all but two agents out of Michigan to keep a lid on the unauthorized landings."

"None around here?" Jay asked, surprised.

"Nah. Not after what you two did to that Grayhawkian battlecruiser." Zed laughed. "That was great, just great. Served the ugly mothers right."

"So, any get through our agents?" Elle asked.

Zed nodded. "That's the reason I woke you two up. A small group of TalkingSticks got through in upper New York."

"TalkingSticks?" Jay asked. "Tall, pencil thin, smell like sand, flat faces and bodies? Those TalkingSticks?" They were always coming through the Immigration Center. Usually they liked to become accountants or lawyers as cover. They had almost no imagination and very little personality. And, as far as Jay knew, had never caused a problem.

Zed nodded. "The same."

"So why do they want the Zahurians?" Elle asked. "And enough to risk a treaty violation?"

Zed only shrugged. "Some ancient grudge, I'm sure. They'll be showing up in your area shortly. We don't know how they're traveling."

"They got a telepath with them?" Jay asked.

"Nope," Zed said. "Not that we know about. They'll be as lost trying to find the Zahurians as you two."

"Thanks," Jay said.

"Don't mention it," he said as he cut the connection.

"Sometimes I wonder why he keeps us around," Elle said, as Jay dropped down into a chair beside her.

"We're the best rookies he's got," Jay said. "That's why."

"So how come we need the devil's help to find some trees?"

Jay shrugged. "Because good ol' Bob thinks like a tree and we don't?"

"Yeah," Elle said. "Maybe you're right."

Jay realized what he had just said. He might not

be able to think like a tree, but he could certainly think like a TalkingStick. And that meant he knew exactly where they were headed.

"Come on," he said, pushing himself to his feet. "We got some thin aliens to stop."

"Trees or Sticks?" Elle asked as she downed the last of her coffee.

"Sticks," Jay said. "We'll let good ol' Bob find the trees."

Fifty minutes later they pulled the LTD up to the side entrance of a small office complex, situated just off the main highway south of Concord. The building had clearly been built in the seventies, with white paint around the roof and wooden siding warped and peeling in a dozen places. Six cars filled the small parking lot, all of them even older than the one they were driving.

The morning had turned hot and even muggier than the day before. This spring had turned into the hottest on record. Walking around in black suits in this kind of weather was about as silly as trying to hike in the Idaho mountains with patent leather shoes.

Jay figured that the least the MiB could do was make the suits more heat resistant for summer, and warmer in the winter. With all the alien technology hanging around, it seemed to Jay that might be possible. But no, these suits were bought right off the rack in New York. Not cheap, not expensive.

Just black suits.

They had been driving with the air-conditioning on high, even though it was early, and neither Jay or Elle really wanted to climb out into the heat and humidity.

"You think they're in there?" Elle asked, staring up at the small office building through the car window.

There were four offices, two on the lower floor, two on the upper. Only the office on the right had the blinds still pulled and the closed sign in the window.

"I know they are," Jay said. He pointed at a white van pulled up behind the right side of the building.

"How do you want to play this?" Elle said. "They may be pissed that we're stopping their little revenge mission."

"Atomizers on stun," Jay said, pulling his pistol out and checking it quickly.

"Yeah," Elle said. "Sounds good."

"Ready?" Jay said.

They both piled out into the heat of the morning. Jay felt as if the suit instantly sucked in the heat and the sunlight, holding it against his body. Someday he'd remember to ask Zed exactly where the idea of black suits came from. And if the guy who started it had died of heat stroke.

Jay motioned that Elle should take the back stairs off the alley and he went up the front. By the time he climbed the single flight of stairs and knocked on the door, he was sweating. Not the public image the MiB wanted, he was sure.

A tall, thin man answered the door, his glasses on his nose, his hair tousled, as if he had just gotten up. "Yes?"

"Hiya, Danny-boy," Jay said, stepping in front of Danny Brandon and forcing him back inside with the point of his Atomizer. "Came to pick up your friends."

Danny Brandon was a TalkingStick who had been living on Earth for the past six years, peacefully working as an accountant, minding his own business as far as MiB records indicated. But aliens stuck together, and Jay had no doubt that the other TalkingSticks would be right here, since Danny was the only TalkingStick in the area.

"I don't understand what you are talking about," Danny said, doing a fairly good job of acting innocent. He had been on Earth a long time.

From the back room there was a loud banging, then Elle's voice said, "I wouldn't try that if I were you."

"Those friends," Jay said. "Remember now?"

Danny said nothing, and a moment later Elle pushed three TalkingSticks through the door and into the front office. The place suddenly filled with the smell of hot sand. Not a bad smell at all. Nothing like what the Grayhawkians had smelled like yesterday, or what Bob had smelled like in Zed's office.

"A flagpole reunion," Jay said, staring at the three tall, thin aliens.

"Danny," Elle said, standing beside the alien in the human disguise. "What exactly did the Zahurians do to your friends here? I'm kind of curious what would make your people take this kind of risk."

Danny spoke in a high, almost silent language to his friends, then turned to Elle. "They ate an entire colony of our people."

"A colony?" Elle asked, sounding as shocked as Jay felt.

Danny nodded. "A ship full of Zahurians ate over sixty thousand of our kind. Alive."

"Wow," Jay said. "That's a lot of breadsticks."

Elle shot Jay a dirty look, then turned back to Danny. "Tell your friends that, by tonight, all the Zahurians on this planet will be destroyed."

Danny nodded.

"And tell them," Elle said, "that we're sending them home without punishment."

"Thank you," Danny said, bowing slightly.

"And you, Danny-boy," Jay said. "We'll deal with later."

Danny nodded, then relayed Elle's messages to the tall aliens standing quietly in the hot office.

Ten minutes later Jay and Elle escorted the TalkingSticks down the back stairs and into Pro's containment van, then climbed back into the wonderful air-conditioning of the LTD.

"Sixty thousand," Elle said as she buckled her seat belt and brushed the sweat from her eyes. "Zahurians are real monsters, aren't they?"

Jay flashed on the paper boy struggling with one

of the trees, then cleared the image from his mind. Maybe it *was* worth dealing with the devil to kill these trees. Just maybe.

He spun the LTD in a quick U-turn and headed back toward the warehouse. They had trees to kill.

The world is divided into people who do things—and people who get the credit.

—DWIGHT MORROW

As the very first rays of the yellow sun lit up the thin layer of clouds, Cistena and Autropur stood, roots hidden in low Earth shrubbery, near a side entrance to the huge human building. Two other Zahurians stood in the same manner on the other side of the entrance, forming what looked to be a normal planting of trees around the door.

A human had parked a vehicle near the entrance and was in the process of opening the door.

"Remain calm," Autropur thought directly to Cistena. "Do not move."

"I will be calm," Cistena thought back. "Do not worry. Just get us inside."

As the human let the door close, Autropur sent a thin root along the ground that grabbed the door and stopped it from clos-

21

ing all the way. As the others inside had said, the human didn't notice. He just walked forward into the faintly lit corridors, not looking back. He would be inside for over an hour. Plenty of time for the Zahurians to get inside and into the large pots that held the Earth trees that looked so similar to them.

They had also been told that there were humans who walked the corridors late at night. But during this time of the day, they didn't come around much, which was lucky for the Zahurians.

"Clear."

The thought came strongly from the Zahurians inside, who could see where the human had gone.

Autropur did a quick scan of the huge open area around the building. Not a human in sight.

Autropur yanked open the door, holding it with a larger root so that the other Zahurian couple could move through. Cistena followed. Within moments, all four were moving along the vast hallway of the building. It was much easier to pull themselves along the smooth surface than the Earth ground, and they all made good time.

Autropur scanned the area. The other Zahurians had been correct. Zahurian-looking Earth trees seemed to be everywhere, standing beside doors, grouped in large numbers in central areas, lining artificial water pools.

The other Zahurians had chosen a location deep inside the building, near the center, where the most Earth trees were kept. Autropur, Cistena, and their two companions moved quickly down the hallway, making sure to not leave a trail on the slick tile floor as they went. The humans might be primitive, but they could track. That much they had proven.

Near the center were six Zahurians, their thoughts buoyant at the arrival of Autropur, Cistena, and the others.

"Find locations," one thought.

"Quickly," another thought.

"What do we do with the Earth trees?" Autropur asked, staring at the pot full of dirt, rock, and an Earth tree the size of a thin Zahurian.

No one answered his question.

Autropur scanned the six already in the pots. They all seemed to be blocking their thoughts. Clearly, the question was expected, and the answer not liked.

"You ate them," Cistena thought, the sharpness of the accusation clear and harsh.

"There was no other choice," one thought back, defending all six.

"At first we simply cut them into tiny pieces and put our roots around them, but there wasn't enough room to hide them effectively, so we absorbed them."

Autropur could feel Cistena's wrath and disgust rising. If she became too upset even the humans' thoughts wouldn't block her presence from the dreaded Nelek.

"We do what we must to survive," Autropur thought at her, making it intense and private, making her stop.

Autropur whipped out a root and cut the Earth

tree in the nearest pot off at the ground level. The tree started to fall, but Autropur's roots and lower branches whipped out, cutting it, collecting the parts, sucking them inside his system. In all his years Autropur had never tasted another plant, but survival came first now. There was no time to question the morality of the act.

Within a moment the tree was gone. Not even a leaf remained on the smooth floor of the building. With a quick motion, Autropur pulled the tree's roots from the huge container and soon they had disappeared as well. Then Autropur thought directly at the shocked Cistena. "Get in and calm your thoughts. The Nelek will come soon."

Cistena started to reply, but Autropur snapped a shield down and turned to a nearby Earth tree in another pot, using cutting roots to tear it apart quickly, as he had done to the first.

Beside him Cistena climbed into the pot and dug her roots into the dirt, smoothing the ground so that it looked the same as the soil around any of the other trees, Zahurian or Earth-type.

Behind Autropur, the other two Zahurians were also making short work of two Earth trees. By the time the human who had inadvertently let them in came back, heading for the entrance, nothing looked out of place.

Autropur was careful not to allow Cistena's anger in. The act had been done. It was past. The Nelek was coming.

"Survival," he thought at Cistena. "Think only of survival."

"At what price?"

"At any price."

Jay and Elle had spent the better part of the afternoon in the war room, taking down the tacks and trying to figure out where the meat-eaters had gone. In the areas with missing people and animals, where Jay was certain they hadn't gotten the Zahurians, he had marked a large circle. Now they drew back and stared at the ten large circles on the wall map, showing the area where the twenty remaining Zahurians might be. A few of the circles overlapped, but not by much. And no pattern emerged to make them dash back out into the spring heat and start a new search.

Jay had just decided to go take a nap and think on it, when the communication board beeped. Elle answered it, and Zed's face filled the screen.

"The last two Zahurians have been destroyed in Michigan."

"Down to ours, huh?" Jay said.

Zed nodded. "Bob is on his way. Work into the night if you have to. Get this over with by tomorrow night."

"More pressure from above?" Elle asked.

"We'll hold most of them back tonight," Zed said. "But by tomorrow, if there's a Zahurian left, your area will be filled with dozens of alien warships a lot harder to destroy than the one you got lucky with yesterday."

"We'll find 'em, boss," Jay said. He didn't feel at

all confident about keeping that promise, but it sounded like the right thing to say at the time.

Zed laughed. "Bob will find them. You just kill them."

With that, the screen went blank.

"It's going to be tough," Elle said, "working with that guy."

"No choice," Jay said. "Wake me when the horned wonder gets here."

No need.

The thought formed clearly in Jay's head, freezing him in his tracks. Just as before, he felt dirty, violated, and angry that someone had climbed inside his head.

"Shit." He glanced back at Elle.

"What?" Elle asked. "What's wrong?"

"He's already here."

"Oh."

Jay sat down in his chair again, facing the map. He would work with this Nelek to kill the meat-eaters. Then he would think twice about this job. Some things just weren't worth it, and this was becoming one of those things very quickly.

Sorry you feel that way.

The thought filled his head as the Nelek entered the room, followed at a good distance by MiB agent Ess.

"Stay out of my head!" Jay said, standing and facing the alien.

"Or what?" the Nelek said aloud as his sewer smell filled the room. His pig face was even uglier than Jay remembered it, and his horns made him look even more like a walking, talking image of the devil.

"We have work to do," Elle said, stepping between the two. Jay was surprised she didn't gag.

"I'm going back to headquarters," Ess said, smiling at Jay and then almost running from the room. Jay didn't blame him at all. He wanted to run just as badly.

"Then why don't you?" the Nelek said aloud.

"Because," Jay said, staring into the depths of blackness in the alien's eyes. "I have a job to do and you're gonna help me do it right, pig-boy."

"Humans," the Nelek said. "So proud. So primitive."

"Our motto," Jay said. "Been thinkin' of havin' it tattooed on my arm."

"This way to the car," Elle said. She pointed to the door and waited until Jay led the way toward the LTD. Ten minutes later, without Jay saying another word, they were headed out to find their first pair of Zahurians, the windows open to help dilute the sewage smell coming off the Nelek, and the air conditioner running at full blast to fight the hot, sticky day.

A wonderful way to travel.

I never did give anybody hell. I just told the truth and they thought it was hell.

— HARRY TRUMAN

"Turn here," the Nelek said from the backseat, motioning for Jay to turn right onto a small farm road.

The thirty-minute drive from the warehouse to this point had been the closest thing to pure hell that Elle had ever experienced. The rotten smell of the alien was making her sick, and she had been used to some really bad smells in her last job. A body ten days dead in one hundred degree heat didn't smell as bad as this scum. On top of that, she had tried, mostly unsuccessfully, to contain and control every thought and focus only on Jay's driving and the road ahead. It was not something she was used to doing, and she was already getting a headache.

Jay swung the LTD down the side road.

22

"Slow," the Nelek said.

Jay slowed, scanning the road on his side while she checked hers. Then she saw them.

"There," Elle said, pointing at two flowering plum trees standing near a fence. They looked thinner than a Zahurian tree, and not as tall.

"No," the Nelek said. "Ahead."

"Real trees," Elle said. "Sorry." She had so wanted a chance to get out of this car that she had made a mistake. She'd have to be more careful.

They slowly passed the two real plum trees and drove for another quarter mile until she spotted the real alien trees. "There."

This time Jay nodded.

The two trees were attempting to hide in a mass of brush and smaller trees, but their flowers were showing above the brush. Not a place two plum trees might grow naturally.

As Jay stopped the car, the two Zahurians took off at a fairly good speed, moving out of the brush toward a large stand of pine trees.

Both Jay and Elle climbed from the car, Phaser rifles set on wide beam.

The Nelek also climbed out.

Stop!

Jay and Elle both turned to the Nelek, but he clearly hadn't intended that thought for them. It was aimed at the Zahurians. The two trees halted, seeming to shiver on their roots. Elle was also shivering from the feeling of that pig-alien in her mind.

"I will take these," the Nelek said aloud, stepping toward the edge of the road.

"I don't think so, horned boy," Jay said. "You find 'em, I cook 'em."

"Yeah," Elle said. She raised her rifle and fired, burning the two Zahurians to ash within only seconds.

How dare you refuse me?

The thought filled her head like air from a tire pump pressing into a balloon. She took a deep breath, letting the pressure drain, then turned and faced the Nelek, gun at her waist pointing at the alien's middle.

More than anything she wanted to pull the trigger, and the pig-alien knew it. But it also knew she wouldn't. At least not yet.

Bob grunted, his face contorted, even more ugly than normal. And that was damn ugly. For a moment she thought he actually might stamp one of his little hooved feet, like a child throwing a fit.

"Next stop, big Bob?" Jay asked, ignoring the fact that the Nelek was angry and Elle was about to shoot the bastard.

Elle smiled at Bob. The image of the angry child inside the rotting alien made her feel better. She moved around and climbed back into the car, placing her rifle on the seat beside her.

Jay shrugged at the Nelek and got in behind the wheel. After a moment the alien climbed into the backseat.

"Which way, Bob ol' boy?" Jay said, staring ahead, hands on the wheel, ready to drive.

"Forward," the alien said.

Jay nodded.

Elle was glad to get moving again so that the breeze would clear out some of the choking smell. She leaned her head out the window like a dog. Where were the wonderful smells of a corpse? Right now she'd trade anything for that.

"The Nelek is close," Cistena thought directly at Autropur, her panic painfully clear.

The huge area around them was full of humans, all coming and going, moving at different speeds, all busy with their current activities. What these animals did in this building, Autropur couldn't tell. It seemed like some sort of religion. The humans went in and out of each place, sometimes leaving offerings, at other times taking offerings. It had to have some meaning and Autropur only hoped he would have enough time to study them.

Six of the ten Zahurians still outside the human building waited by the entrance for it to get dark, so that they could enter. Four were still greater distances away.

"You know what to do," Autropur said to Cistena. "Full mind screen. No thoughts must escape. We must become like one of the Earth trees around us. Let the humans' primitive thoughts protect us from the Nelek."

Suddenly the image of the Nelek flashed through the thoughts of all of the Zahurians, relayed from the two now facing him somewhere farther away.

Stop!

The power of the Nelek command was greater than Autropur could have imagined, and the Nelek was more hideous than Autropur had been led to expect. The evil animal seemed to stare through anything.

Cistena panicked.

Autropur wrapped a comforting thought around her, holding her with his mind.

Then, just as suddenly, the human wearing black sent searing waves of heat and blackness at the two Zahurians, cutting off the link.

"They are dead," Autropur thought to Cistena. "Now, close your thoughts to all, including me."

"Are we to die?"

"Not if we don't allow a thought to escape," Autropur thought back. "Now, full mind screen."

Autropur waited until he felt Cistena's mind screen fit into place, then put up his own, concentrating inward, so that no stray thought would leak out.

The other Zahurians did the same. For a moment, Autropur felt confident that the Nelek would not find them here, among all these humans with their minds so carefully screened.

Around them the humans moved, paying no attention to the deadly situation developing in their midst.

After twenty more minutes of driving with the Nelek in the backseat, Jay desperately wanted to hang his head out the window like Elle was doing. Anything to get some fresh air. Thank heavens he hadn't had much for lunch. He would have lost it by now.

Elle looked pale as she leaned even farther out the window than before, letting the wind whip her hair around her face and blow the stink away.

They were headed toward a large shopping area near Concord. Another five miles and they'd be in the city itself.

"Turn now," the Nelek said.

Jay swung the car to the left, the only direction he could turn, down a dirt road leading up to a farmhouse. The Nelek said nothing, so Jay drove all the way up to the white home and red barn and then stopped.

"Ahead," the Nelek said.

"No more road," Jay said, shutting off the engine and piling out of the car with relief. At the moment walking seemed like the best idea in the world.

A farmer opened the front door of the house. He was an older guy, wearing bib overalls and a tee shirt. He saw Jay holding a rifle and slammed the door again.

Jay flicked open his phone, taking a few steps away from the LTD to get some clean air. "Pro."

"Yeah," Pro's voice came back clear and strong.

"How far behind us are you?"

"Two minutes."

"Going to need some help," Jay said. "Hurry it up. Got a scared farmer here."

"Understood," Pro said. "Shutting down phone lines and cutting power to that area."

Jay clicked off the phone and nodded to Elle as the Nelek climbed out of the backseat.

"Two near here," the Nelek said, seeming to stare up into the sky. "All the others gathered nearby, also."

"In one place?" Elle asked.

"I cannot tell, exactly," the Nelek said. "Too much interference from human thought. But yes. Together."

Jay laughed. "I usually complain that not enough humans are thinking."

The Nelek looked at him with its dark eyes and said nothing.

At that moment the farmer opened his door, shotgun in hand, and stepped out. "You are on private property," he shouted, brandishing the gun. "Please leave."

Jay glanced at Elle, then at Pro's containment truck entering the driveway.

"You or me?" Elle said.

"Better be you," Jay said.

Elle nodded and put her gun on the roof of the LTD. She put on her sunglasses, then raised her hands, neuralyzer hidden in her palm, and started toward the old man on the front steps. "Sir, I need to talk with you for a moment. We're from the CIA. We're not here to hurt you."

Jay put his gun down, too, to make the old guy feel better.

"Why do you bother?" the Nelek asked.

"What?" Jay asked. "To disarm the farmer?"

"Yes."

"He's one of those we're sworn to protect," Jay said, without looking at Bob. "From the scum of the universe. You know, aliens like you."

When Elle got close enough, she nailed the farmer with her flashy-thing. The old man lowered his shotgun just as Pro slid the truck to a stop and Partner and the Captain piled out.

"Treat him well," Elle said to the containment crew as she headed back to the car. "And I don't know if there are more inside. Careful."

"Wow," Pro said, waving his hand in front of his face as he passed Jay. "Sewer line break?"

"You might say that," Jay said.

They headed past the farmer's barn and across a newly-planted field, slogging through the soft ground toward the tree-line. Jay led the way, with the Nelek following. Ten paces behind him and ten paces upwind, Elle followed. Jay's head was clearing from the smell, and his headache was fading.

"Which way?" Jay said, as they got near the fence line that surrounded the field.

"Continue ahead," the Nelek said.

Jay climbed through the barbed-wire fence and started into the trees, watching for the purple flowers that would indicate a Zahurian. He didn't much like being this deep in brush, especially after seeing what a Zahurian could do up close, but he didn't have much choice.

"Jay?" Elle said behind him.

Jay turned around and almost burst out laughing. Bob the Nelek had gotten his robe caught in the barbed wire, and was having trouble getting through.

"Superior intellect doesn't always get you where you want to go, does it?" Jay asked the Nelek.

The alien only glared at him.

Elle took a deep breath and held it while she moved up beside him, putting her foot on the fence and holding it down while the alien got his robe loose and crawled through.

"You find such a situation amusing?" the Nelek asked as he straightened his robe.

"Normally, no," Jay said, turning his back on the Nelek and heading forward into the brush and trees.

"You hate me that much?" the Nelek asked.

Jay laughed. "What's to like?"

"I help your kind rid yourselves of the Zahurians."

"I doubt you're doing it for us," Jay said. "You're just like the other three dozen races in orbit, wanting a piece of the Zahurians for your own reasons."

"Very perceptive," the Nelek said.

"Even one of these Earth trees could have figured that out," Jay said, pointing at a pine tree beside him and then glancing back at the alien.

The Nelek paused for a moment and stared at the pine tree. "This species has no intellect."

"My point exactly."

Jay plowed on ahead through the brush and trees until finally the Nelek said, "Slow."

Jay brought up his Phaser rifle. "How far?"

"Twenty of your paces," the Nelek said.

Suddenly Jay felt as if every muscle in his body were frozen. He could only move his eyes, and those only enough to see that Elle, now beside him, also seemed frozen.

"Let us loose!" Jay shouted, but nothing but grunts came out of his throat.

I will have my meal.

The thought formed clearly in Jay's mind as the Nelek disappeared into the low brush, leaving Jay and Elle stiff and alone amid the trees like the Tin Man in the Wizard of Oz.

The scum was going to eat a Zahurian! Jay couldn't believe it.

Beside him, Elle made an odd guttural sound, trying to say something.

"I will cut your heart out and fry it," Jay shouted, but the words were only a low squawk.

Laughter filled Jay's mind, then the words, *Do you not find this funny, human?*

Jay had to admit, he didn't.

Not in the slightest.

It is not what they take away from you that counts—it's what you do with what you have left.

—HUBERT HUMPHREY

Thirty-six Troons sat around the circular fixture in the center chamber of the huge warship as it orbited the primitive planet called Earth. All thirty-six stared at the images in the crystal blue water in the middle of the chamber. Under the surface was the Great Head, seemingly looking at all thirty-six of them at the same time. Of course, because it was the Great Head, it *was* looking at all of them.

The Troons were small, almost humanoid creatures who all wore striped brown shirts with images floating across the fronts. Unlike humans, however, they had sandpapery skin, sharp, needle-like fingers, and a smooth, green covering on their flat heads. In the center of each head was a circular hole, black and unprotected. No Troon would ever think of covering his head, not

23

even by accident. But during formal occasions, small flags were stuck into the holes, showing respect for the Great Head.

"One Zahurian," the Great Head said, its head hole pulsating clearly in the water-image. "One."

All thirty-six nodded at the same moment, in the same way, as if attached to one string.

The Troons had not signed the treaty that protected Earth, yet many of their mortal enemies had. A dozen of those enemies now had warships in orbit around Earth, just as the Troons did. But all wanted one thing: a Zahurian.

And revenge.

One Troon broke from the circle and stood, bowing to show its head hole to the image of the Great Head in the water. In truth, the Great Head was thousands of light years away, on the home world of the Troon. But the communication device in the great circle made it seem as if the Great Head was on the ship.

This Troon was not the leader of the ship. No Troon was. It was just his time to speak for the thirty-six.

"Yes?" The Great Head did not call the Troon by name. The Troon had no name. To the Great Head, all Troons were equal servants.

"Proper channels are being accessed, to avoid war," the Troon said.

"How long?" the Great Head asked.

"One full round," the Troon answered, bowing slightly. "It will take the same amount of time for a telepath to arrive to track the Zahurians."

The Great Head was motionless. Then it said, "No longer. I do not care about war with the primitive humans. Only a Zahurian."

"Understood," the Troon said and sat down, taking up a position identical to the rest in the large room.

All thirty-six Troons bowed at exactly the same moment, knowing why the Great Head so wanted a Zahurian to keep and torture. The Zahurians had eaten the thirty-six who parented the Great Head. It had been a great tragedy, which had led the Troon to a short war with the Zahurians. It had ended in stalemate. Failure. It was never spoken of.

Now revenge against the few was their only course.

The Great Head vanished from the pool and all thirty-six Troons stood, moving back to their posts without a word.

Below the great Troon warship, the planet Earth waited to be invaded by the massive number of alien ships in orbit. Only a very few humans even knew the ships were there.

To those in orbit, whether humans knew they were there or not made no difference. Only the chance of battle with other advanced races who wanted the Zahurians for themselves kept the uneasy peace, and kept many of the ships in orbit.

It would be a peace that would not last long.

The thirty-six Troons knew that, and would be prepared when the time came. Other than the honor visited on them by the Zahurians, the Troons had never been beaten, very seldom compromised, and never took prisoners.

At least, that was what they believed.

Jay fought with every ounce of his strength to get loose, but nothing moved. Every time he tried to shout, he could do no more than grunt. Beside him Elle let out an inarticulate moan. She was fighting as well.

He had never felt so totally helpless. And he hated it, more than he had ever hated anything.

His body had always been there for him. Now, it was gone.

Ahead in the brush, Jay could hear the Nelek moving forward. More than anything he wanted to strangle the sewer smell right out of the pig-faced monster.

With that thought the sound of laughter filled his head again. No one should be allowed to crawl inside another's head without permission.

Certainly no alien.

In the brush the thrashing stopped. The humidity seemed to close in around Jay. A mosquito buzzed against his nose, making it itch, making his need to scratch the greatest, most important need in the world.

He needed to scratch.

But he also needed to kill the Nelek. The rot-smelling alien had crawled inside his head once too often. Jay was going to make him pay.

Think!

Itch. His nose itched.

No, think.

Get control.

Itch. No, damn it! Forget the itch!

He forced himself to take a deep breath to calm down. Wait! He was breathing.

He took another breath.

Yes, he was breathing, which meant he still had control of his body. He wasn't completely frozen. His heart was still pumping, he was breathing, he could grunt. Those were all good things.

He forced himself to calm down, not think about his nose itching, and look at his situation.

Think.

Not itch.

Think.

He was standing, one foot forward, facing the brush where the Nelek had gone. His Phaser rifle was level and also pointed forward, his finger hovering frozen over the trigger.

If he could move a finger, just a finger, he would scratch his nose.

No! he told himself. Stop.

Think.

Calm, he repeated over and over, forcing the thought of the itch down into the background.

Stay calm. Wait, do not think. That was the problem. He only needed to focus.

Calm.

Focus on the finger.

Relax.

Focus on the finger. Feel it closing.

Focus.

Calm.

Feel it.

Close it.

Focus.

Close it.

Calm.

Close it.

Suddenly the brush in front of Jay burst into flame as his finger moved just far enough to pull the trigger on the Phaser rifle.

"Yes!" he tried to shout, but the sound was still a strangled grunt.

Beside him Elle grunted, too.

The brush closest to them was vanishing in a whoosh of flame and smoke. Soon more and more was devoured as the Phaser rifle, set on wide burn, cleared a path the size of a road.

Suddenly Jay could see the Nelek, wrapped in the embrace of a Zahurian, gnawing on its trunk with sharp, beaver-like teeth. The tree's acid sap covered the pig's ugly face, dripping from his mouth like saliva. Jay had no idea why the sap didn't eat through that ugly skin, but it didn't.

The Nelek chewed.

Bit into the trunk.

Chewed some more.

Green saliva dripping off his chin.

The Phaser burned a path toward the Zahurians and the Nelek, but none of the three aliens moved.

Clearly the Nelek had the trees frozen also. Bob seemed to be in some sort of drugged state brought on by the taste of the Zahurian sap. He was glassy-eyed and smiling as he chewed.

The sight made Jay want to throw up.

The Nelek bit again, chewed.

The Phaser burnt right at them.

The Nelek didn't move.

He just kept chewing.

It was going to be his last meal if he didn't move soon.

He didn't.

The Phaser beam tore off the Nelek's right arm and burnt most of the Zahurian to ash.

The instant the Phaser blast touched the Nelek, both Jay and Elle stumbled forward, completely able to move again. It felt so good, Jay wanted to dance right then and there.

Until inside his head he heard the scream of the Nelek.

A scream of pain.

Of anger.

Elle pulled up her rifle.

They didn't dare allow that alien's anger to become focused on them. It would fry their brains faster than a Phaser burnt a Zahurian's flowers.

Jay turned the Phaser on the pig-faced alien, just as the one-armed devil turned toward them.

Elle's Phaser blast caught the Nelek just as Jay felt the impact against his mind, like a huge fist gripping his conciousness. Then it was gone.

The energy of Elle's shot sent the Nelek and what was left of the two Zahurians into a massive cloud of ash and smoke.

It was like a bad movie where the devil vanished in a cloud of smoke and the stink of sulfur. Except that the Nelek had vanished in a burst of fire and sizzling flesh sounds. The smell was still that of a New York City sewer backing up on a hot summer's day.

"He was eating the Zahurians," Elle said, amazed. "No wonder he wanted to help us find them."

"You all right?" Jay asked.

"Yeah," Elle said. "Lucky we escaped. Good job." Elle flipped open her phone. "Pro, we got some cleanup and fire problems here."

She nodded at what she heard from the other end and flipped the phone closed. The she looked at the pile of ash that remained of the Nelek. "So now what do we do?"

"Enjoy the walk back to the car," Jay said.

"Why?" Elle asked.

"Because we can," Jay said. "Because we can."

I always view problems as opportunities in work clothes.

— HENRY KAISER

It took Cistena moving a lower branch in the Zahurian sign of listening before Autropur dropped his mental shields. Around them, many humans were moving, since the sun had barely cleared the middle of the skylight in the building over their heads. What was Cistena thinking, moving a branch like that?

"The Nelek has been killed," Cistena thought. Autropur felt almost overwhelmed by her joy.

"How?" Autropur asked, wanting to believe Cistena, but not able to shake the feeling it might be a trick.

"Two more of our kind were also killed," Cistena replied and Autropur heard the agreement of the others, all of whom had lowered their mental shields. "The humans

24

wearing black killed the Nelek as he feasted on our companion."

Autropur knew it was no trick. The images of what had happened flowed through him from the Zahurians inside the human building, and those still outside, waiting to get in. The Nelek was truly dead.

Relief flooded through Autropur's sap. The Nelek was dead. The humans had killed it.

"We are saved," Cistena thought.

But Autropur knew instantly that Cistena was wrong.

They were not safe. They had only escaped the Nelek. Autropur quickly pressed that thought through the excitement around him, forcing the others to calm down, to think.

"What should we do?" one outside asked.

Autropur scanned the area inside the building, and the other earth trees that looked exactly like them. There was no safer place on the planet.

"Come inside tonight."

Elle sat beside Jay, facing the communications screen. Zed fumed. It was almost seven in the evening, and the sun was low in the sky outside the warehouse. This conversation was the third one they had had with their boss since they had killed the two Zahurians and the Nelek. Elle still hadn't shaken the feeling of the monster crawling around inside her head, freezing her muscles. And she knew she would have nightmares for years about the Nelek, green saliva dripping from its mouth, eating the Zahurian with such relish.

During the first conversation, Zed hadn't been able to believe that the Nelek had used his telepathic abilities to freeze them. He had said things like, "I'll kill the bastard."

And, "I knew better."

Elle didn't want to ask what he meant. Figured it was better to let some things be known only to the boss.

Then, when they had finished their report with the part about killing the Nelek as he ate the Zahurian, Zed calmed down. "Bastard deserved it."

Back at the warehouse, Zed had asked them for a full report again. Clearly he was explaining something to someone, somewhere.

Now, Zed was back on the communication link talking about the remaining problem, the one Jay and Elle had talked about all afternoon. How would they find the last sixteen Zahurians?

"Let me tell you, hot-shots," Zed said, moving his face up close to the camera, making it appear that his head had suddenly gotten bigger. "We've got until this time tomorrow evening to find those trees."

"How many ships are coming in?" Elle asked. She didn't really want to know. There were so many races out there that the Zahurians had pissed off, more than likely it would be an alien convention.

"More than can fit in the entire state of Connecticut," Zed said. "No containment possible."

"How about sticking a huge flashy-thing on a satellite," Jay asked, "and after they get the Zahurians and leave, we flash the whole place?"

Zed looked at Jay with disdain.

"Sorry," Jay said, shrugging.

"We're going to have an interstellar war in Connecticut and you're making jokes," Zed said. "Chances are it will destroy the planet. And you know something? Not one of those bastards up there would care."

"We'll find the trees," Jay said.

"That we will," Elle said. "But we could use some help."

"None available," Zed said. "I've got every agent chasing the unauthorized landings of the little fish trying to sneak in tonight. I should be able to send you help tomorrow morning."

"Please?" She knew they were going to need all the help they could get.

Jay only nodded.

Zed frowned at them. "Don't just sit there," he said. "Get going. You've got less than twenty hours to find sixteen man-eating trees."

"No problem, boss," Jay said, saluting.

"Another joke?" Zed growled.

Jay shrugged. "Yeah."

"You used to be funny," Zed said, and broke the connection.

"Pressure," Jay muttered. "Too much pressure."

"That's okay, Tiger." Elle patted his hand and stood. "I never thought you were funny."

The end of the human race is that it will die of civilization.

—RALPH WALDO EMERSON

Pro, Captain, and Partner stood next to the MiB containment van in the Burger King parking lot as Jay and Elle parked beside them. Pro wasn't eating, but both Captain and Partner were sucking down burgers and fries like there was no tomorrow.

Which, if they didn't find the Zahurians, might well be the case.

Jay grabbed a fry from Partner and slumped against the van while Elle headed inside to get a soft drink. The last three hours had been as frustrating as the three previous days. They had scoured the area where the Nelek had said the Zahurians were gathering, but not one of the purple-flowered aliens could be seen.

Partner offered Jay another fry, but he refused. "Watchin' my figure."

25

Captain only snorted.

They stood together in the warm evening air, not talking, four men in black suits and ties, leaning against a black truck.

Jay didn't need a Nelek to figure out that they were all thinking the same thing.

Where could sixteen alien trees hide?

But no answers were forthcoming, even from all that thinking. If they didn't find some answers quick, they were all going to be out of a job.

And Jay didn't even want to think about how many millions of people would die in the alien battle to find those sixteen meat-eating Zahurians.

Elle came back outside and leaned against the bumper of the LTD, facing the four men while she worked on her soft drink. She looked as troubled and deep in thought as they did.

"So," she said, finally. "How come all the Zahurians were moving to this area?"

Exactly what Jay had been wondering. Some of the alien trees had to have traveled a long ways, in a very short number of days, to get here. Why?

No one answered Elle's question, so Jay said, "We find that answer, we find sixteen meat-eaters."

"Well," Elle said, sweeping her arm out to encompass the night and all the commercial buildings around the Burger King. "The answer is around here somewhere. They came here for a reason. We're just not looking in the right place."

"Or for the right thing," Pro said.

Jay looked at Elle for a moment, then at Pro, who smiled. "Watch out, boys," Pro said. "The kid has an idea. I can see it coming."

"You readin' my mind again?" Jay asked.

"Who would want to," Elle said, "after that Nelek crawled around in there?"

"Not funny," Jay said.

"Truth is seldom funny," Pro said.

Jay held up his hands in surrender.

"So give us the idea, hot-shot." Elle reached over and stole one of Captain's last fries.

"We quit looking for the trees," Jay said.

All of the agents around him stared at him, as if he'd lost it.

"And we start looking for hiding places," he continued. "How many places can hide sixteen flowering plum trees?"

"A lot," Pro said.

Elle nodded. "But I think Jay's got something there. We don't just look for *any* hiding place, but one that would draw the trees from long distances. A really *safe* place."

"Exactly," Jay said. "We set up a search pattern of this entire area tonight. List every place we see, both from the car and on foot. Then, with some help tomorrow morning, we search 'em all."

"Long night," Pro said, "but it might work."

"It has to work." Elle sounded determined. "Pro, enlarge us a map of this area and let's get started."

By sunrise, none of them had seen a Zahurian, but they had listed over two thousand places where the aliens might hide within a twenty-square-mile–area.

And they were all hungry.

Betty's Fine Restaurant on the outskirts of Concord was open twenty-four hours a day, so they met there as the sun shot orange and red through the clouds blanketing the sky.

Betty's was a place that made you feel comfortable right off the bat. It was filled with plants, cloth-covered booths, and a long counter. A rack of freshly-baked pies greeted Jay as they entered, and his stomach rumbled at the wonderful smell of coffee and frying bacon.

Zed had said that containment crews and more agents would be pouring into this area in less than two hours. It had been a hell of a night holding off the entire universe, but somehow, Zed and the others had managed it. From the reports Jay got, six alien ships had been destroyed, and hundreds of different aliens captured and deported.

Jay hoped he and Elle would have as much luck.

He watched as Elle talked the morning restaurant manager—a thin, motherly woman named Carol—into letting them have the back room that was normally used for banquets. Carol set all five of them up with coffee, took their orders, and then got out of their way.

Pro spread the map out on the big table, and together they started throwing out possible Zahurian hiding places.

All active warehouses were tossed out first. Nowhere for trees to hide safely.

All parks. Agents had already found a number of the aliens in parks and would be likely to look there.

Any wild or forested area. Same reason.

All active greenhouses. Not safe for the trees because humans might move them into the open.

After fifteen minutes they had the list carved down to two hundred old warehouses, hidden ravines, and small valleys that couldn't be searched by chopper. It was going to take a lot longer than ten hours, even with one hundred agents, to search all those locations.

Jay was getting discouraged.

All of them were.

And none of it felt *right*. It was as if they were still missing the most important piece of the puzzle.

Jay dropped down into a chair and stretched out his feet just as Carol came in with the coffeepot.

"Breakfast is almost ready," she said. "Sorry for the delay. Got busy out there."

"Not a problem," Elle said, staring at the map.

"What's the matter, good-looking?" Carol said to Jay while refilling his cup. "Not finding what you're looking for?"

"Got that right," Jay said.

Carol moved to refill Pro's cup. "You know," she said, "when my kids and I used to play hide-and-seek, the hardest places to find them were always out in the open."

"Yeah," Captain said. "I remember that. Drove my friends nuts with that trick when I was a kid."

Jay glanced at Elle. His fellow agent was staring at Carol, her mouth open. Then her gaze turned to the hanging plants.

"Jay," Elle said. "You seeing what I'm looking at?"

Plants, right out in plain sight. Where no one would pay any attention to them. "Sure am."

"Do you think . . . ?" Elle asked.

"You just might be right," Jay said. "Anythin' on that list that would make them travel so far?"

"Nothing," Elle said. "Nothing on this list."

"I agree." Pro gave Carol a big smile as she filled his cup. "I think you're going to get a big tip."

"Glad to help," she said.

Jay stood and moved up to the manager. "We need a little more help. Do you have a phone book we could borrow?"

"Sure," Carol said. "White or Yellow Pages?"

"Both."

"Be right back." Carol disappeared.

Jay motioned for Partner to help her, then leaned over the map. "All right, where is plain sight in the area we covered last night?"

"A bunch of places," Elle said. "The parks we ruled out."

Jay shook his head. "Doesn't feel right, unless there are a lot of regular flowering plum trees there."

"None of the parks we looked at had any," Pro said.

"We didn't see any, either," Elle added.

Pro frowned. "Then, large commercial areas?"

"Like a shopping center?" Elle said.

"Or a mall?" Jay was studying the map. Inside the twenty square miles they had covered last night there were a number of malls and shopping centers, some large, some not so large. All of them had plants in the parking lots, from what he could remember. And if they had them in the parking lots, more than likely there were plants inside, too. Anyone who took the time to beautify a stretch of asphalt would surely take more care with the interior of a building.

Partner returned then, dropping the phone books on the table. Jay grabbed the Yellow Pages and flipped them open to "Commercial Flowers and Plants." There were three major listings.

He nodded to Pro. "Find the owners or managers of these places. Wake 'em up. Find out where the largest number of flowerin' plum trees are located. Commercial groves, decorations, greenhouses full of the damn things. You know what I mean."

Pro yanked out his phone.

Captain took the second listing.

Partner, the third.

All three moved to a different part of the large banquet room full of tables and sat down.

In the meantime, Jay and Elle looked up the names and addresses of all the malls and shopping centers. There were a bunch of them.

"I'll take that one," Jay said, pointing at the listing that read, *Bridgeport Mall—Largest in the Area*.

Elle nodded. "I'll take Wentworth Mall."

Jay nodded. Under the Wentworth listing it said, *Sixty Retail Shops*.

When Carol came back carrying breakfasts, she found four men and one woman, all dressed in identical black suits and ties, spread out around the room at different tables, all talking on black phones at the same time.

She shook her head, put the breakfasts down in front of each of them, and left. The food was cold by the time the agents even thought of touching it.

> *I used to believe that anything was better than nothing. Now I know that sometimes nothing is better.*
>
> —GLENDA JACKSON

Pro stood next to Jay, munching on a piece of cold bacon, smiling. It was the first time in hours that any of them had even thought of smiling. But at the moment, Jay was feeling the same way.

"Thank you for your help," Jay was saying to the mall manager on the other end of the line. He clicked the phone closed and looked at Pro. "You first."

"Bridgeport Mall," Pro said.

"Bridgeport Mall," Jay said, giving Pro a high five.

Elle finished her own call and turned to the two men. "No flowering plum trees to speak of."

Captain clicked his phone closed and grabbed his coffee as he crossed the room. He, too, was smiling.

26

"Anything?" Elle asked him.

"Bridgeport Mall," Captain said.

Both Jay and Pro laughed. Elle looked at them like they had lost it.

"So, gentlemen," she said. "You want to fill me in on the joke?"

"Bridgeport Mall," Jay told her. "Full of hundreds of flowering plum trees."

Elle groaned. "You're kidding?"

"Nope," Jay and Pro said at the same time.

"I heard the same," Captain said, laughing.

"So what are we waiting for?" Elle asked.

Jay pointed over his shoulder at Partner, who was still talking with someone. "Might be other sites."

"The guy I talked to said no," Captain said. "Only Bridgeport used flowering plum trees, at least in this area."

Pro nodded. "The nursery I talked to said the same thing."

"So," Elle said, "if our idea of them hiding in the open is right, they are in that mall."

"Would explain why they traveled so far," Jay said.

Elle smiled. "That it would."

Partner hung up his phone and turned to look at them.

"Well?" Pro said.

"Guy at Honeytown Nursery said the only place for flowering plum trees in this area was the Bridgeport Mall."

. . .

Bridgeport Mall would normally have been a fifteen-minute drive from Betty's Restaurant, but Jay made it in six minutes and fourteen seconds, even though the traffic was getting bad with the first part of the morning commute. Not since he and Kay were chasing the bug had he been in the LTD at those speeds, in that much traffic. He even passed one cop, but by the time the cop even had time to react, Jay, Elle, and the LTD were long gone.

Jay stopped the car near the south entrance to the mall, where about twenty other cars and a bus were already parked. He picked a spot that was out of the direct line-of-sight of the glass doors.

"People here this early?" Jay glanced at his watch. "It's only a little after seven."

"Staff?"

"Maybe. But a bus?"

"Well," Jay said, "if there are people in there, then we need to go undercover."

Elle nodded. "Find out what we're up against."

"Right."

She climbed out of the car and took off her coat, then pulled off her tie and flipped up her collar. Tugging her shirt out of her pants, she tied the two tails in a knot across her waist, leaving it loose in the back.

"Amazing," Jay said, standing in the open parking lot beside her, watching the transformation. She had gone from looking staunchly conservative to almost sexy in two seconds flat. Even the shoes seemed in style.

She put on her sunglasses, ruffled her hair, and then said, "How do I look?"

"I doubt any tree's going to recognize you," he said. "I almost don't."

"Good." She reached into one of the compartments inside the car and pulled out an earplug, sticking it in her ear. It was a two-way communication link with the unit in the LTD. That way she could let Jay know if she got in trouble.

"Meet me on the other side," she said. "I'll do a straight walk-through."

"Careful," he said. "Give 'em room if they're in there."

"Oh, don't you worry about that," she said, smiling. "I've got no intention of arm wrestling one of those trees."

She headed toward the door. Jay watched until she was inside, her arms swinging as if she didn't have a care in the world. Then he climbed back in the car and drove to the other side of the mall, giving the glass doors a wide berth.

He heard nothing from her for four long minutes.

Four very long minutes.

Then suddenly she appeared on the other side of the building. Her face was white and she looked very tired. The light spring was gone from her step.

She dropped down into the passenger seat of the LTD. She was sweating. Jay flipped on the air-conditioning.

"Well?" he said.

"A nightmare." She took a deep breath. "I thought I had walked into a nightmare."

Behind them Pro pulled up in the containment van. Jay motioned for him to hold on a minute, then turned back to Elle. "Are they in there?"

"I think so," she said, seeming to gather herself. "There have to be five hundred flowering plum trees in that mall, most in big, round planters, a bunch in the central area. There's one every twenty feet, throughout the entire place."

"Oh, man," Jay said.

Elle nodded. "It's like walking through a forest of the monsters. All of them are the right size, right shape, all have flowers. A nightmare."

Now Jay understood what had rattled her so much. After a week of hunting these killer trees, walking through what seemed like a forest of them would have rattled him too. It gave him chills just thinking about it.

"Any possible suspects?"

She nodded. "A bunch in the very center of the mall have thicker trunks, and their flowers are just a little deeper purple than the others. Looked like there were about sixteen of them, too, but I didn't stop to count, that's for sure."

Jay nodded. "And the people in there?"

"Mall walkers," Elle said.

"Mall walkers?" Jay had never heard the term before.

"Yeah," Elle said. "Maybe a hundred of them,

mostly elderly, all with tennis shoes and funny hats, walking circles around the inside of the place."

Jay knew he still looked puzzled, because Elle added, "Exercise. Walking. You know? Staying fit?"

"Oh." Jay shook his head. People walked around malls like they were big indoor tracks. Weird. "So why the hats?"

Color was finally returning to Elle's face. "I think it's some sort of mall-walker uniform."

"Oh," Jay said again.

He glanced at the huge building. It felt right that the alien trees would hide there. Without some luck, and a chance comment by the Nelek, they never would have thought to look inside. And Jay doubted any of the other aliens in orbit over the planet would have either. Maybe there was a reason these meat-eaters were hated and feared by half the galaxy. They were smart.

Now the question was, how to take them out?

He punched a button on the dashboard communication link and a screen dropped down. A moment later Zed's face appeared.

"Tell me you found them."

"We might have," Jay said. "Bridgeport Mall."

"They're all at the Bridgeport Mall?" Zed asked.

"We think so," Jay said, and Elle nodded agreement.

"How the hell did they get inside?"

"We don't know," Elle answered. "But there are a lot of regular flowering plum trees in there."

Zed nodded. "Good work."

"So," Jay said, "help comin'? Or do we go in alone?"

"Six containment crews in twenty minutes." Zed checked something in front of him. "Four more agents and a dozen more containment units in two hours."

"Can't wait that long." Elle frowned. "The mall will be open. We've got mall walkers in there already."

Zed punched some keys on his desk. "Wait for the other containment units at least. I'll see what I can do."

"Okay," Elle said. "We'll go thirty minutes from now."

"Well," Jay said, "you ready to do some plannin'?"

"When you are."

The two of them got out of the car. Pro, Partner, and Captain were standing beside the truck, waiting. They had thirty minutes to figure out how to save Earth.

They had to make the best of each minute.

Autropur watched the human walk past them. This one wasn't like the rest of the humans who walked the corridors right after the sun came up. This human seemed younger, dressed differently, and wasn't wearing a head covering. None of the other humans seemed to pay it any mind, but that meant nothing to Autropur. There was something about this particular human that bothered Autropur.

The human did not slow its pace as it walked away. All the other humans seemed to move much more slowly than this one. And all the others came past the center of the mall many times in a morning. Autropur noted that this one human seemed to be intent on looking around, as if it hadn't been in the corridor before. It wasn't until the human was some distance away that it dawned on Autropur what was wrong. The human wore black pants, black shoes, and black eye guards, just like the ones the deadly humans wore.

A slight shiver of panic shook the flowers on Autropur's stems, but he soon calmed himself. If this human was like the ones in the hats, it would return shortly, moving in the other direction. If not, Autropur would warn the other Zahurians.

A time passed. The human did not return.

Autropur became convinced the human was a member of the dangerous group covered in black.

"We must prepare to fight," Autropur said, directing a clear thought at the others. "We have been discovered by the humans who wear black."

The flowers on the others shook, as his had done. Yet after a short time, all waited for Autropur to tell them what to do. There were only sixteen of them left on the evil world called Earth. Autropur had become their leader, a duty he had not wanted. But survival came first.

If survival was possible.

"We must act first," Autropur said to his companions. "It will be our only hope."

The others said nothing, continuing to wait for guidance.

Over the last few days Autropur had noted that a number of the human enclosures surrounding their location contained weapons the Zahurians could use in a fight with the humans. But Autropur knew that without shelter from the heat of the human weapons, they would have no time to use their own weapons. And nothing could stand between those human heat weapons and the Zahurians except other humans. So Autropur told his fifteen companions to study the movements of the humans around them.

After they had done so, Autropur told them what each would need to do.

No one objected. Not even Cistena. They all knew that following Autropur was their only hope for survival.

A slim hope, but still a hope.

Time will teach more than all our thoughts.

—BENJAMIN DISRAELI

The Great Head appeared in the shimmering pool in the main control room of the large Troon warship orbiting the primitive planet Earth. The thirty-six Troons who ran the ship had summoned it. They now sat in chairs around the shimmering pool.

The thirty-six bowed as one as the Great Head appeared, remaining bent forward so that the Great Head could see the holes in the flat, green surfaces of their heads.

The Great Head showed the hole in the top of its head to the thirty-six who sat around the pool, then said, "You need my wisdom?" Its voice was soft, gentle, soothing to the thirty-six.

One of the Troons stood and bowed slightly before speaking. "We need your wisdom," the Troon said.

27

"Then ask," the Great Head responded.

"We have intercepted a private message sent between the humans. The message states that the humans have found the remaining Zahurians."

"Are they destroyed?" The Great Head's voice was now so powerful that it seemed to fill the huge room with the force of the question.

"Not yet. But soon."

"Do the other races in orbit with you know of this?"

"No," the Troon said. "It was an accident that we discovered it."

"Accidents happen for a purpose," the Great Head said. "Do you know where the Zahurians are located?"

"Yes."

"Then bring me a Zahurian before the humans destroy them all."

"War may result," the small Troon said.

"Understood," the Great Head said. "Bring me a Zahurian."

"We will do so."

The Troon sat down again, taking up the same position as the other Troons, blending in with the thirty-six perfectly. No member of the thirty-six would ever look or act differently from the others. One spoke for all. All acted as one. It was the way of the Troon.

The Great Head bowed slightly, its giant head hole pulsing. Then it vanished.

The Troons stood as one and moved back to their stations, stepping as one.

In a short time, the giant Troon warship dropped suddenly from orbit, flashing toward the surface of the planet before any of the other warships had time to react.

It had started.

Research had faxed Pro a floor plan of the Bridgeport Mall in the containment truck. Now they spread the plans out on the hood of the LTD and studied them. Elle pointed to where she thought the Zahurians were located: the central court. Just thinking about going back into that forest made her shudder.

A dozen of the shops leading onto the court had back doors, and if they had had a dozen agents, that would have been the best way in. But the way it stood now, Elle figured their best bet was to get the mall walkers out of the way first, hopefully without alerting the Zahurians that anything was wrong and then go in and zap the aliens to ash.

Near the end of each wing of the building, the mall walkers were in areas that couldn't be seen from the central court. The rescue effort would start by having the containment crews extract the walkers as they made their way into those corridors.

The containment crews would then seal all the mall entrances and watch all store exits.

Elle would go in through the department store that emptied onto the center court. She would have good cover in there and might be able to get close to their targets.

In the meantime, Jay would work his way up from the south entrance. With luck, the walkers would all be gone and he and Elle could catch the Zahurians in a crossfire.

At least that was the plan. Elle liked it, especially considering how little time they'd had to come up with it.

All at once, six black containment trucks pulled into the mall parking lot and stopped near Jay and Elle.

"Give 'em their assignments," Jay said to Pro. "And tell them to wait for our signals before moving."

Pro nodded. "Understood."

At that moment Jay's phone beeped in his jacket pocket: a signal from Zed that something important was happening.

Jay jumped into the driver's side of the LTD while Elle slid into the passenger seat. By the time Jay got behind the wheel, Zed's worried face was already on the small screen.

"Troon warship headed right for you."

"What?" Elle said.

"How'd they find this location?"

Zed only shrugged. "Telepath, maybe. Who knows? But they're headed your way fast."

"How long do we have?"

"I'd be looking up," Zed said, "in about thirty seconds."

"Shit!" Jay ran his palm over his face.

"Any weaknesses?" Elle asked, her voice amazingly steady. She wanted to panic, but forced herself to think.

"They're stupid," Zed said. "Try the same trick you pulled on the Grayhawkians if you can. I doubt they were paying attention. They don't think humans exist."

"Understood," Jay said.

Zed cut the connection.

Jay and Elle both bailed out of the car, Phaser rifles in hand, looking up at the clear sky.

"Pro!" Jay shouted. "Incoming warship!"

"Everyone grab a Phaser rifle and follow our lead!" Elle added. "Spread out around the parking lot."

Instantly seven MiB containment crews, twenty-one agents who were more used to cleanup duty than fighting, had dispersed throughout the parking lot, rifles in hand, finding cover where they could. They were trained and knew exactly what they were doing. They just didn't do it as often as Jay and Elle.

Then, just as Jay figured things couldn't get any worse, things did.

Behind them, the door of the mall slammed open and half a dozen elderly people in bright orange hats came streaming out, screaming.

Elle grabbed one man by the arm. "What's going on?"

"Trees," the old guy said, his eyes wide with fear.

"What did the trees do?" Elle shouted. Overhead the sky started to darken.

"They moved," the old man said between gasps for breath. "Grabbed a bunch of the walkers. Won't let them go."

Elle nodded and released him. The old man kept running.

"Hostages," Jay said.

"Looks like the Zahurians know we're here." Elle looked up at the bottom of the huge Troon battlecruiser now blocking out the morning sun. "Wonder if they know about the Troons?"

"At the moment," Jay said, staring at the ship over them, "that's the least of our problems."

Elderly people in bright hats continued to stream out into the parking lot, only to look up and run back inside. Elle doubted many of them would live through the next hour—though not because a tree ate them, or they got shot by an invading Troon. With all this excitement, she was betting on half a dozen heart attacks.

She just might have one herself.

Autropur waited until each Zahurian had a human firmly in its grasp, then climbed out of the pot and moved toward one of the human shops. He was the only Zahurian to not take a human hostage. The rest of the Zahurians followed, dragging their humans along with them. With two roots he yanked on the metal grating that covered the entrance to the shop, bringing it down.

Every Zahurian was taught, at a young age, to throw the Cutting Disk. It was a most deadly weapon.

Autropur moved inside the shop and picked up a few thin, round platters. He dropped one to the floor and it shattered. Silicon material. A form of glass. The edges were blunted, not sharpened, but thrown with enough speed, they would still cut through most anything. With a quick flick of a branch, one disk flew at a human standing on the other side of the central court.

The human seemed to be calling out to another one being held by a Zahurian. Possibly a mate.

The disk flew true and fast, just like a real Zahurian Cutting Disk. It sliced the human below the head, stopping the flailing motions of the human limbs as the head rolled sideways, eyes wide, mouth open. The disk smashed against the stone wall as the human slumped to the ground. A true Cutting Disk would have severed the head easily. But these weapons would clearly do enough damage.

Autropur was pleased with the throw. It had been years and the practice was well-remembered.

Some of the hostages started jerking and moving about, but Autropur paid them no heed.

"Cutting Disks!" Cistena thought, joy filling the message. "An entire room full of Cutting Disks. We can defend ourselves."

"Good throw," others thought.

"They are blunt, but they will work if thrown hard enough," Autropur thought in response. He gestured around the room. "Other weapons are here." With one root he picked up a metal knife and threw it at a nearby wall. It stuck.

Again Cistena's joy filled his thoughts as she saw their chances of survival increasing.

"Six of you gather weapons and place them against the stone wall near where we stood."

Six agreed, glad for the weapons and the fact that Autropur had a plan.

"Another five give your hostages to others and follow me."

All did as Autropur said, and within a few moments they were moving benches to the location near the stone wall. And then they moved earth trees, pots and all, to the same location, until the earth trees formed a thin barrier in front of the wall. There was enough room for the sixteen Zahurians to get behind the barrier with their human hostages.

"Shelter," one said to Autropur.

"Yes, it is our only hope. We will hold the humans until a ship comes to take us home," Autropur thought. "Otherwise, we defend ourselves to the death."

Silence greeted this.

Then Cistena filled the silence. "It is a good hope."

The others agreed and went back to work bringing weapons and hostages to the bunker they had built. It was war.

Nobody is ever ready for anything. If they were ready for it, there would be no point in living through it.

— DAVID GERROLD

Twenty-one MiB Special Forces containment agents and Jay and Elle stood ready, Phasers in hands, spread out around the huge parking lot of the Bridgeport Mall, watching as the Troon battlecruiser settled to the ground just slightly before eight in the morning, eastern time.

The ship was shaped like a giant doughnut, with a hole through the center, and it was green. But whether it was made of a green metal, or painted green, Jay couldn't tell. As with the Grayhawkian ship, it seemed to float silently in the air, even though this ship was big enough to slip over the Empire State Building like an engagement ring.

Jay leaned across the hood of the LTD, Phaser aimed at the ship, watching, waiting

28

for any opening in the green metal. He knew they had gotten lucky with the Grayhawkians.

The doughnut-shaped ship settled to the parking lot without extending landing gear, crushing a dozen light poles as it did so. That was the only sound the landing made. Creepy to watch, that was for sure. Jay wasn't used to something that big moving that silently.

Just inside the doors of the mall, a large group of elderly mall walkers stared in disbelief as the ship landed. Jay felt for them. Moving trees behind them, a huge spaceship in front of them. Luckily, they were either all going to die shortly, or none of them would remember this in an hour. Jay hoped for the latter.

Inside the LTD, Elle read faster than she ever had in medical school as reams of data about the Troon race spewed across the monitor. She was desperately looking for any detail that would help them in the impending fight.

Nothing. Or at least, nothing obvious. The Troon were a powerful and strange race. A hive mentality, but each Troon was an individual. They called their leader the Great Head.

As the ship settled to the ground, she hopped out of the LTD and joined Jay, Phaser tilted across the hood of the car.

"Anything?" Jay asked. "They must have a soft spot on that ship somewhere."

"Nope," Elle said. "The ship seems to have no

weakness. And there's thirty-six of them in there. No more and no less."

"Great," Jay said. "Just great."

For ten very long minutes the ship remained silent.

Finally Jay grabbed his phone from his jacket pocket and called Zed.

"Any more ships comin' in?" he asked when Zed answered.

"They're all holding orbit for the moment," Zed said. "It's a giant game of chicken up there."

"Let's hope they keep playin'," Jay said.

"Yeah," Zed said. "One starts firing and we're all dead. Troon ship down?"

"Yup," Jay answered. "The doughnut has landed."

"Those goofballs never do anything alone," Zed said. "Keep that in mind." He cut the connection.

"Will do," Jay said into the dead phone before he flipped it closed and turned back to Elle. "All holdin' orbit for the moment. And Zed said the Troons always do things together. Know what that meant?"

"Hive mind," Elle said. "But without a hive, or much of a mind, from what I could tell. They have no leader inside the ship, yet all of them lead. That's what the background info said."

"And all follow?" Jay asked.

"Seems that way."

Jay stared at her for a moment.

She shrugged. "Like I said, they're a weird bunch."

"I'm gathering that," Jay said.

At that moment a section of the doughnut spaceship split open and a long, gently-sloped ramp lowered toward the mall. The bottom of the ramp ended about twenty feet from the west entrance.

The mall walkers inside panicked, but didn't bolt. They couldn't run forward now. And they couldn't go back to the trees. They were trapped.

"Get ready," Jay said, aiming his Phaser at the ramp. "It's showtime."

From their angle Jay and Elle couldn't get much of a shot up into the ship, but Pro, Captain, and Partner were all closer, with better shots at the inside.

A moment later all thirty-six of the Troons came marching down the ramp toward the entrance of the mall, goose-stepping in their brown uniforms like actors in a bad war movie.

"That all of them?" In all his years as a cop in New York, Jay had never seen anything so silly. And he had seen a lot of weird stuff.

"Looks like it." Elle shook her head. "Yeah. Six rows. Six Troons per row."

"Take 'em out!" Jay shouted.

Almost instantly, a dozen Phaser beams cut the marching morons apart, leaving nothing but a smoking mass of brown uniforms on the ramp.

"Hold your fire!" Jay yelled. A brown cloud drifted on the morning breeze.

"No more in there?" Jay asked, looking at Elle.

"Nope," Elle said. Then she started laughing.

Jay and Elle walked across the parking lot to the

ramp and looked up inside. A moment later Pro joined them. He couldn't help laughing, either.

"Got any idea what to do with this?" Jay asked, pointing at the ship.

"Tow truck," Pro said. "We'll dump it where we dumped the Grayhawkian ship. Into the sun."

"Do it quick. Might discourage the rest of those ships in orbit from going up against us." Jay grinned. "We're two for two."

Pro nodded, slapping him on the shoulder. "I wouldn't want to try for three."

"Yeah," Jay agreed. "Haul that thing away and see if you can buy us time to clean up the mess inside the mall."

Pro headed for his truck at a run. Around the mall the other containment crews started escorting the elderly out of the doorways where they had been hiding. Shortly, they would be getting new memories. A lot of people around this area would be getting new memories, Jay figured.

Jay stared at the mess on the ramp, then shook his head. "Superior intelligence?"

"Very," Elle said.

"Glad I'm stupid," Jay said.

"Yeah," Elle said. "Me, too."

Jay didn't exactly know how to take that.

Thirty minutes later, Pro and Zed had managed to get a friendly ship to lift the Troon ship up and out of sight. Zed said they weren't going to toss this one into the sun, but he he wouldn't say what they were going to do with it. Jay figured that more than likely it went to an enemy of the Troon who now owed Earth a really big favor. Zed was great at doing things like that. From what Jay had heard, Zed's ability to trade favors was one of the main reasons Earth was running the way it was, and hadn't been taken over by some profit-hungry alien race.

Three more containment crews had arrived, and the local police were helping block the streets around the mall, even though none of them knew why. They had orders. And new memories.

All the mall walkers were out of the mall except for the fifteen hostages. Almost every tree must have its own hostage, Jay guessed.

Those poor people were not having a good morning. All they had done was go to the mall for some exercise, never expecting to be kidnapped by angry alien flowering plum trees. Which would screw up anyone's morning.

"Help has arrived," Elle said as MiB Agents Gee and Ess pulled their LTD up beside Jay and Elle's. Gee always reminded Jay a little of Kay, with the square jaw and graying hair. Gee had been with MiB for twelve years, and before that a Ranger, Special Forces, in the Army. He was the best shot of all the MiB agents. Jay had never seen him even smile, let alone laugh. One serious mother. Jay had once made a wager with another agent to see who could get Gee to smile first. Neither of them had succeeded. Jay figured a smile would crack open Gee's face.

Ess was the opposite. He was short, balding, and had a slight gut pushing out the front of his black coat. He laughed a lot, and talked even more. He had been a cop in California, then joined MiB eight years ago after his entire family was killed. Jay liked Ess, but wouldn't want to be partnered with him. The guy liked opera, and thought he could sing the stuff.

"Found the last of them, huh?" Ess asked as he approached the floor plans of the mall spread over the hood of the LTD.

"Trapped inside," Elle said. "They have elderly hostages."

"The plan?" Gee lifted one eyebrow.

Now that they had two more agents, they had revised the plan. "Two of us go in through the department store on the east side," Elle said, pointing at the floor plan. "Two down the south corridor."

"Containment holds all the other doors," Jay added.

Ess smiled. "Crossfire. Might work. I like it. I really like it."

"Skylight?" Gee asked.

Elle nodded. "Big one."

"One of us needs to be up there," Gee said. "Clean line of fire."

"If we can get shots without hurting the hostages," Elle put in.

"There are no others," Gee said.

Jay turned from the map, his gaze taking in the sprawling mall building. "You gentlemen ready?"

Both nodded.

"Corridor, roof, or department store?" Elle asked.

"Corridor," Ess said.

"Roof," Gee said.

"Firing position in ten minutes?" Elle asked.

All nodded.

Without another word the four agents turned and headed for the mall, carrying their Phaser rifles across their chests.

Jay could feel the adrenaline rushing through his body as he and Elle walked through the warm morning air toward the back entrance to the department store. It felt almost too good.

But it was always this way, whether you were a cop or an MiB agent. Days and days of boredom, punctuated by a few minutes of excitement—and terror. At the moment, Jay didn't want to give up that life for anything, whether the bad guys were the perps on the streets of New York, or the scum of the universe holed up in a suburban mall.

All the containment agents were in place, covering the exits. Jay nodded to Elle before they went in.

They had a plan.

And they had big guns. What more did they need?

Those whom war has joined together, let no peace put asunder.

— JAMES FRANCIS BYRNES

The smell of the perfume department almost choked Jay as he and Elle crept toward the center court of the mall. He hated perfume. In his New York cop days, he had tended to stay away from women who wore too much of it.

He moved closer to the store entrance and crouched beside a glass case, looking through the metal gate at the mall beyond. From his vantage point, all he could see were empty tree planters. No sign of the Zahurians. In the distance, regular flowering plum trees stood in front of the closed shops. At least, he hoped they were regular trees. There were a whole lot of them.

The place was silent, as if the air pressure were holding any noise down. From what seemed like a vast distance, Jay could hear

29

someone sobbing, but he couldn't see where the sound came from.

Elle had moved around to the front wall of the department store and opened an electrical panel. The store manager had told Elle how to raise the metal gate that protected the store during off hours. Jay had argued against raising the gate, since the bars might offer some protection from the Zahurians. But Elle had told him that the metal would scatter their Phaser shots, more than likely putting the elderly mall walkers in danger.

So the gate was coming up. As soon as everyone was in position.

Jay pressed his lapel, where a small mike was hidden inside the cloth of his shirt. The mike would send whatever he said to the earpieces of all the agents inside and outside the mall.

"In position," Jay whispered. "Can't see any Zahurians." He didn't know why he was whispering. The trees sure couldn't hear him. In the oppressive silence, it just *felt* like he should whisper.

"I'm short of my position," Ess said. "This place is creepy."

Elle glanced at Jay and smiled.

"The aliens have built a blockade of Earth trees and humans," Ess went on, "against the stone wall to your left. I can't get any closer without being seen."

"I'm at the skylight," Gee said. "No clear shot. We have one casualty near the center court. Elderly woman. Looks like her neck was slashed. Pieces of a smashed plate are scattered behind her body."

"Plate?" Jay said.

"Plate," Gee said. "Her throat must have been cut by it. Those things can be deadly if thrown hard enough."

"Shit!" Jay whispered.

"Got that right," Ess said.

"Are the other hostages alive?" Elle asked.

"Yes," Gee said. "From what I can see."

Jay looked over at Elle, who pointed up, indicating they should raise the gate. In the department store, the two of them were stuck in a position where they couldn't even see the enemy, let alone get a shot.

By moving against that stone wall, the trees had again shown how smart they were. That was the easiest location to defend, and the hardest for the MiB agents to attack. And from the sounds of it, they had weapons now. Or, at least, a bunch of place settings.

"Gate coming up," Jay said. "Be ready for anything."

Elle punched the button and the gate ground upward, filling the empty mall with a low rumbling noise.

For a moment nothing happened. Then, when the gate was about four feet off the floor, the world around them shattered.

Literally.

Plates were coming in under the gate faster than bullets, seemingly hundreds of them at the same time. Jay could only see them when they smashed against something, sending glass shrapnel every-where.

Both Elle and Jay hit the floor and covered their eyes as display cases shattered, mannequin heads were knocked off, even windows on the other side of the store were broken.

"Shut that thing!" Jay shouted to Elle over the incredible din as tons of glass smashed around them.

Somehow, Elle managed to punch the button that reversed the gate, bringing it down until the last few plates shattered against the closed screen.

Then even that stopped.

Again, quiet settled over the mall. But Jay's ears were still ringing.

The entire attack had lasted less than fifteen sec-onds.

Around them, the department store was ruined. What seemed like a million bottles of perfume had been smashed, filling the air with a thick, putrid smell and covering the floor in yellow pools. Mir-rors were torn half off walls, clothes were ripped on their hangers, even the wood walls were dented and splintered in places.

"You two all right?" Ess asked in Jay's ear. "Sounded like world war three."

"Okay," Jay said. "You ought to have heard it in here."

"Yeah," Elle said. "What the *hell* was that?"

"The trees were whipping dinner plates at you with their roots and branches," Ess said. "Like in-credibly fast Frisbees."

"Where'd they get the plates?" Elle asked.

"A glassware store right beside them," Gee answered. "They have an almost unlimited amount of ammunition there, and each tree can whip five or six plates at the same time, very accurately."

"Machine-gunning plates," Jay said. "What will they think of next?"

"Let's hope we don't find out," Elle said.

"Meet at the cars," Jay said. "We need a new plan."

"Agreed," Gee said.

"On my way," Ess said.

On the way out, Jay almost slipped and fell in a huge puddle of perfume as he tried to pick his way over more broken glass than he could ever remember seeing in one place. It wasn't until he and Elle got outside that either of them noticed they had been cut in half a dozen places. Their suits were cut and sliced in even more places.

Ess took one look at them and whistled. "Imagine if one of those plates had hit you. Wow."

Gee, on the other hand, turned to one of the containment crew members and shouted "Medic!"

Right then and there, Jay decided he liked Gee more than Ess. A whole bunch more.

Autropur calmly thought "Stop" as a few of the Zahurians kept throwing disks at the now-closed gate.

"We pushed them back!" Cistena said, joy filling the thought.

Autropur let the others join in the short celebration. The truth of how Autropur felt was quite different. The humans had been pushed back, but they would not remain that way for long. They would not allow the Zahurians to stay in this location until help arrived. Autropur also thought now that help would never arrive. It had only been a hope. Not a reality.

"Eat to celebrate," Autropur thought at the others. "Only two of the hostages."

"Will we have enough left to protect us?" Cistena asked, excited.

"We do," Autropur said. "We might as well have full streams during the coming fight. We came to this planet to eat, did we not?"

All agreed, then quickly picked two of the hostages and pushed them forward. These two were the heaviest, with the most fat on their frames. Good choices for a meal.

With roots whipping, the Zahurians quickly sliced up the two humans and passed the pieces around, sucking the wonderful meat and bones into their roots.

Autropur took one human limb, cut it quickly into smaller pieces, then sucked it inside. A moment later Autropur blocked the joyous thoughts of the others so that the enjoyment of the animal fat in his system could be fully savored.

A vast feeling of contentment flowed from all the Zahurians in those moments. Autropur was glad for them. After all, a last meal should always be savored.

And a human meal should be savored even more, considering it would be humans who killed them.

It took the four MiB agents twenty minutes to come up with a new plan. Zed had given them permission to kill the hostages along with the aliens if they had to. The official position of MiB was that losing a few humans to save the planet was worth it.

Zed said he personally thought that "stunk." But they were to do what they had to do to wrap up the Zahurian situation, as he called it, as quickly as possible.

Time was running out.

A full-scale interstellar war was about to break out right over their heads.

Still, none of the agents wanted to kill hostages, so they tailored their plan to save them.

Twenty-six minutes after retreating from the department store, the four agents were back inside the mall. This time Ess was on the roof, taking up a position to cut down the Zahurians from the skylight if the human hostages were taken out of the picture.

Elle took a bullhorn and moved into position just down the south corridor from where the Zahurians had made their stand. She was out of the line of fire unless she moved forward, around the corner of a brick wall. She was going to talk to the hostages, and try to get them to help save their own lives.

Gee and Jay, the two best shots, were in the west corridor. On their stomachs, they had crawled from one normal Earth flowering plum tree to another, using the huge pots for cover.

Jay felt like he was crawling through a nightmare. He kept looking up, expecting a Zahurian to be leering down at him—if a tree could leer. But every time he looked up he saw regular old flowering plum trees. It still felt like a nightmare. And no matter how hard he tried, he couldn't wake up.

Finally, about seventy paces from where the corridor merged into the central courtyard, Jay and Gee stopped, positioning themselves in small alcoves. If each of them looked around the corner of the wall in front of them, they would both have clear shots at the Zahurians across the court, about a hundred paces away.

On their backs they had carried folding stools, the kind parents took to soccer games to sit on while their kids played. Jay quickly opened his and made sure it locked, solid enough for him to stand on.

Across the corridor Gee did the same.

They both climbed up on the foot-tall stools at the same time, testing the stools' strength and position.

"Ready," Jay said into his lapel, leaning his back against the stone wall. He checked his Phaser rifle to make sure it was on tight beam.

"Ready," Gee said.

"In position," Ess responded.

"Tight beam, Gee," Jay said.

"Check."

"Go ahead, Elle," Jay said.

"Attention!" Elle shouted through the megaphone, her voice echoing in the eerie silence. "Attention, those who are being held by the trees."

"We hear you!" one man answered, his voice desperate. "Get us out of here! They're eating us!"

Several others responded also, making an unintelligible racket. But they were all clearly in a panic.

Jay glanced over at Gee, who only shrugged. There had been more than one casualty. Seems the Zahurians had had a morning snack.

"Calm down! and listen!" Elle shouted. "Those trees are aliens. They can't hear like we do, so they don't know what I'm saying to you!"

The hostages calmed a little, but Elle shouted through the megaphone again. "Listen, everyone. I'm trying to save your lives! Shut up!"

The babbling from the hostages stopped.

"Good." Elle's voice echoed down the corridors like the Wizard's voice in the Great Palace of Oz. That movie had nasty trees, too, which threw apples instead of plates. But Jay still liked the movie.

"When I reach the count of three," Elle said, "I want you all to duck. Or at least lower your heads. Then, if you feel the tree let go of you, run!"

The only response was a confused murmuring from the hostages, and one woman crying louder and louder.

"Go for it, Elle," Jay said into his mike.

"One!"

The word seemed incredibly loud in the empty halls.

"Two!" Elle went on. "Remember, duck and run!"

The hostages were dead silent. Jay just hoped that in a moment they wouldn't be dead, period. He gripped his rifle and nodded to Gee.

"Three!"

"Duck!"

At that moment, both Gee and Jay eased their shoulders around the alcove walls and leveled their rifles on the group of trees across the courtyard. Because they were standing on the stools, their rifles were about seven feet in the air. If the plan worked, they would cut off the top third of all the Zahurians, right above the humans' heads.

Both opened fire at the same moment, before any of the trees even knew they were there.

Gee started from the right.

Jay started from the left. He let his Phaser's beam linger just long enough to cut through everything, all the way to the wall behind the aliens, before sweeping it forward.

Between the two of them, Jay and Gee cut the tops off of a bunch of Earth flowering plum trees, and sixteen Zahurians.

Green sap splattered against the wall.

Elderly mall walkers were running from the grove of shortened trees like ants. Some of the sap had hit them, burning holes in their clothes and exposed skin.

Above the center court, the window broke as Ess opened fire from the roof, his Phaser set on a wider beam as the hostages cleared out.

Jay and Gee just kept firing, using their tight beams to trim more and more off the Zahurians, one clip at a time. Jay knew how a barber must feel.

Cutting.

Cutting.

Cutting.

Suddenly, a plate smashed into the wall above Jay's head as a few of the Zahurians, even cut down three feet, fought back. More plates shattered against the walls, sending both Gee and Jay back into the safety of the alcoves.

Plates smashed into the skylight, temporarily stopping the firing from above.

More humans were running from the shortened trees, heads down, pumping elderly legs faster than Jay imagined most of them had run in years. The green sap ate at their shoes, pants, and mall-walker hats.

"All hostages on the ground or clear," Ess said.

Jay kicked his stool out of the way and dropped to one knee as another plate smashed into the wall over his head. Diving, he rolled behind a planter, brought up his rifle, and started cutting the trees off two feet above the ground. He just hoped that any hostages left on the ground wouldn't suddenly get the idea to jump to their feet.

Gee was also on one knee in the alcove, firing away.

A few more plates smashed against the walls. Then they stopped.

"Cease fire!" Ess cried. "Stay in positions. Elle, shout for those people to run!"

Elle's voice again sounded through the mall, pumped out by the megaphone. "You people on the floor. Get up and run! Now!"

Three mall walkers did as they were told, jumping to their feet and running away. None of the trees tried to stop them.

"All clear," Ess said as he opened fire from the skylight again. This time his Phaser was on full beam.

Jay flipped his Phaser to normal and burned the area, moving forward as he fired. Beside him, Gee did the same.

Smoke poured from the site of the Zahurian last stand as the MiB agents turned them into ash.

The entire area was covered in green sap, eating into the walls and flooring. It was going to be a mess for containment.

"They're all gone," Ess said.

Jay stopped firing and flipped open his phone. "Zed?"

A moment later Zed's voice came back. "Go ahead, Junior."

"All Zahurians destroyed."

"Hot damn," was all Zed said, and the phone went dead.

Jay laughed as he put the phone away.

"Zed like that news?" Gee asked, watching as Ess finished off a last Zahurian branch with a few short blasts of Phaser fire from the roof. Down the corridor, Elle was rounding up the hostages and sending them toward the containment crews and ambulances outside.

"Does a 42nd Street hooker like thousand dollar bills?" Jay asked.

"I don't know," Gee said.

"Trust me," Jay said. "Zed liked the news. I'm pretty happy with it myself."

"Yeah," Gee said. "So am I."

Then Gee smiled. Jay stared in amazement for a moment. Gee had smiled. And his face didn't break or nothin'.

A person is really alive only when he is moving forward to something more.

—WINFRED RHOADES

Six hours after it ended, Elle had called Jay para-noid, and he was starting to believe he was. But somehow, he just didn't feel sure it was over. Something wasn't finished. He could sense it. He just didn't know what "it" was.

The containment and cleanup of the mall had taken the entire day, even with almost two dozen containment teams and a total of six agents. This mall wasn't going to reopen to the public or the mall walkers for at least a week.

Elle had spent most of the afternoon at the hospital, helping the crew there make sure all the mall walkers had their stories straight, thanks to a flash or two from the neuralyzer.

The official story was right out of the nightly news. It seems a lone gunman from

30

New York had come into town and killed and burned four mall walkers while on a drugged-up rampage early in the morning. He'd even tossed acid on several others. The FBI had shot him, and an "official" investigation was continuing.

Zed had told them that most of the alien warships in orbit had left. Only a few remained in a standoff to see who would leave last. But now that the Zahurians were dead, Earth held no interest for them. Zed was very happy about that.

Jay spent the afternoon with Pro and his team in the mall, going through the Zahurian remains. The longer he worked, the more Jay became convinced that not all the aliens were in that final battle. He was even starting to believe that one or two of them might have slipped away, and were hiding among the hundreds of other trees still in the place.

After the main cleanup was done, he spent an hour walking from one flowering plum tree to another, carefully jabbing each with a large, sharp stick. Finally, after covering one wing of the huge place, he went to Pro.

"Security camera in this place?"

Pro nodded. "The kind that constantly tapes over itself every twenty-four hours unless something happens," Pro said. "No one ever looks at it, normally. I pulled today's tape and locked it up. Replaced it with blanks." Then he laughed. "Somehow that evil, drugged-up terrorist must have shorted the security system, including the videos, when he broke in."

"Cute," Jay said. But he wasn't laughing. "Can I look 'em over? The real tapes?"

Pro shrugged. "I don't see why not."

Pro led the way to the van. The day was another hot one and the inside of the van was stuffy, even with the air-conditioning going. Pro showed Jay how to fast-forward and slow-motion the tape, then sat back, out of the way.

Jay watched the trees take the mall walkers hostage.

He watched the woman begging for her husband's release get cut down.

He watched the attack with the plates.

He fast-forwarded through the trees eating two of the hostages.

He ran the last battle in slow motion.

None of the trees could have escaped being cut down and burned. That much was clear. Sixteen trees went in, sixteen trees were destroyed by Phaser fire.

Elle joined them in the truck when she found out what he was doing. "You're being paranoid."

"Yeah," he said. "Just can't believe we're done. If there were forty-two trees at this drop site, we got 'em all."

"I'm glad we're done, personally."

Jay nodded, smiling. "I'm gonna be jumpin' for years at the sight of any purple flower."

"You're not the only one," Elle said. "How about dinner? Pro, you and the team almost free?"

"We are at that," Pro agreed. "How about Betty's? We never did finish breakfast."

"Great!" Elle said. "Jay?"

Jay wasn't paying attention, for his own words had suddenly come back to haunt him. They had always been fairly certain that forty-two trees were in that first drop. And Jay could account for every one of those forty-two Zahurians' deaths. Fine. But why did the Zahurians do the first drop here? In this area? Where there was a mall with hundreds of flowering plum trees? "Seams."

"What?" Elle asked.

"Seams," Jay said. "They came here first because they discovered this seam in our security net. Right?"

Elle nodded, looking confused.

Jay pulled out his phone. "Research."

"We're never going to eat, are we?" Pro shook his head sadly.

Elle shrugged. "Not a clue."

"Go ahead, Jay," the voice on the other end of the line said.

"I need reports of missing persons and pets around the Bridgeport Mall in Concord for the last five years. Anything within a mile. Fax 'em to Pro's truck."

"On the way in a moment," the voice said and then the phone went dead.

"Remind me to go meet those people in research some time," Jay said as he put his phone away.

Elle nodded. "Jay, what are you thinking?"

"Paranoid thoughts," Jay said.

"You really think that there might be more Zahurians here?"

Jay nodded. "Yeah. And maybe in other areas, too."

"That thought doesn't get out of this truck," Elle said. "Not by phone or any other way. We tell Zed, only in his office, only with his office sealed up tight. We don't want those ships back in orbit because you can't leave well enough alone."

"Agreed," Jay said.

Elle looked at Pro.

He raised his hands. "Not a word out of me."

At that moment the fax machine started.

Twenty minutes later it stopped.

"I'll be damned," Elle said after scanning the reports.

"Paranoid, huh?" Jay said.

It seemed that every six months, almost like clockwork, someone went missing in this area. And it had been going on for years and years. Clearly, this mall was one of the regular Zahurian stops in the dinner cruise around the galaxy. This was just the first time they had been caught. Jay would wager there were a lot of other missing persons and animals over the years at the other drop sites, as well.

Zed was going to be pissed. And there was no doubt that Jay and the rest of the MiB agents would be stopping to check out flowering plum trees for years to come.

"Pro," Jay said. "Get containment on all sides of the mall."

Elle laughed. "Let me guess. There's about to be

a terrible disease that strikes all the flowering plum trees in the Bridgeport Mall."

"Wiped every damn one of them out," Jay said, shaking his head in mock horror. "Just awful."

Suddenly he felt a lot better. He knew he was going to feel even better when the flowering plum trees in that mall were all piles of ash.

Pro turned from his keyboard. "Containment in place. But after this, can we have dinner?"

"I'm in the mood for something light. A salad?" Elle asked, laughing.

"No salad!" Jay said, remembering the image of the Nelek eating the Zahurian, green saliva dripping down his face.

"Nope," Pro said. "Just steak. Big, red, juicy steak."

"A man after my own heart," Jay said. "Now, let's go kill some plum trees."

ABOUT THE AUTHOR

DEAN WESLEY SMITH is an award-winning editor and best-selling writer. He has sold over thirty-five novels and hundreds of short stories under varied names. Besides his own novels, he has written books in the worlds of *Star Trek, Spider-Man, X-Men, Aliens, Predator, Shadow Warrior,* and others. He has won a World Fantasy Award and a Locus Award and been nominated numbers of times for Hugo Awards, Nebula Awards, and Stoker Awards. Currently he is writing full-time and editing the *Star Trek* anthology series *Strange New Worlds* for Pocket Books. He lives on the Oregon Coast with his wife, writer and editor Kristine Kathryn Rusch.

They are the pinnacle of evolution, the universe's perfect killers...

ALIENS ™

ALIENS, BOOK 1: EARTH HIVE by Steve Perry	____56120-0 $4.99/$5.99 in Canada
ALIENS, BOOK 2: NIGHTMARE ASYLUM by Steve Perry	____56158-8 $4.99/$5.99 in Canada
ALIENS, BOOK 3: THE FEMALE WAR by Steve Perry and Stephani Perry	____56159-6 $4.99/$5.99 in Canada
ALIENS: GENOCIDE by David Bischoff	____56371-8 $4.99/$5.99 in Canada
ALIENS: ALIEN HARVEST by Robert Sheckley	____56441-2 $4.99/$6.99 in Canada
ALIENS: LABYRINTH by S.D. Perry	____57491-4 $4.99/$6.99 in Canada
ALIENS: MUSIC OF THE SPEARS by Yvonne Navarro	____57492-2 $4.99/$6.99 in Canada
ALIENS: ROGUE by Sandy Schofield	____56442-0 $4.99/$6.99 in Canada
ALIENS: BERSERKER by S.D. Perry	____57731-X $4.99/$6.99 in Canada

**Buy all the *Aliens* novels on sale now wherever
Bantam Spectra Books are sold, or use this page for ordering.**

Please send me the books I have checked above. I am enclosing $____ (add $2.50 to cover postage and handling). Send check or money order, no cash or C.O.D.'s, please.

Name _____

Address _____

City/State/Zip _____

Send order to: Bantam Books, Dept. SF 8, 2451 S. Wolf Rd., Des Plaines, IL 60018
Allow four to six weeks for delivery.

Prices and availability subject to change without notice.   SF 8 1/98

Aliens™ © 1986, 1997 Twentieth Century Fox Film Corporation. All rights reserved.
™ indicates a trademark of the Twentieth Century Fox Film Corporation.

The adventures continue in

ALIENS™ *vs.* PREDATOR™

One is a race of ruthless and intractable killers, owing their superiority to pure genetics. The other uses the trappings of high technology to render themselves the perfect warriors. Now, the classic conflict of heredity vs. environment, nature vs. nurture, is played out in a larger—and bloodier—arena: the universe.

ALIENS VS. PREDATOR: PREY ___56555-9
by Steve Perry and Stephani Perry $4.99/$6.50 in Canada
ALIENS VS. PREDATOR: HUNTER'S PLANET ___56556-7
by David Bischoff $4.99/$6.50 in Canada

And don't forget

PREDATOR™

The ultimate hunters have landed. Drawn by heat and the thrill of the chase, these alien warriors have one goal in mind: to locate the ultimate prey.

PREDATOR: CONCRETE JUNGLE ___56557-5
by Nathan Archer $4.99/$6.50 in Canada
PREDATOR: BIG GAME ___57733-6
by Sandy Schofield $4.99/$6.99 in Canada

- -

Buy all the *Aliens vs. Predator* novels on sale now wherever Bantam Spectra Books are sold, or use this page for ordering.

Please send me the books I have checked above. I am enclosing $___ (add $2.50 to cover postage and handling). Send check or money order, no cash or C.O.D.'s, please.

Name _____

Address _____

City/State/Zip _____

Send order to: Bantam Books, Dept. SF 9, 2451 S. Wolf Rd., Des Plaines, IL 60018
Allow four to six weeks for delivery.
Prices and availability subject to change without notice. SF 9 1/98
Aliens™ © 1986, 1997 Twentieth Century Fox Film Corporation.
Predator™ © 1987, 1997 Twentieth Century Fox Film Corporation. All rights reserved.
™ indicates a trademark of the Twentieth Century Fox Film Corporation.

Come visit

BANTAM SPECTRA

on the INTERNET

Spectra invites you to join us
at our on-line home.

You'll find:

< Interviews with your favorite authors and
excerpts from their latest books
< Bulletin boards that put you in touch with
other science fiction fans, with Spectra
authors, and with the Bantam editors who
bring them to you
< A guide to the best science fiction re-
sources on the Internet

Join us as we catch you up with all of Spectra's finest
authors, featuring monthly listings of upcoming titles
and special previews, as well as contests, interviews,
and more! We'll keep you in touch with the field, both
its past and its future—and everything in between.

Look for the Spectra Spotlight
on the World Wide Web at:

http://www.randomhouse.com

SF 30 1/99